“We can’t do this.”

Carter tried to push Mallory away, but his heart wasn’t in it, nor was the rest of his body.

“Yes, we can,” she said, breathing the words into his ear. “We *are* doing it.”

“No, no we shouldn’t...oh, God,” he said as she darted her tongue between his lips and seized his mouth again.

She nibbled her way along his jaw. “Why shouldn’t we?”

“You don’t really want to is why,” he panted as her lips reached his neck. “It’s just the moment. It’s the night and the Christmas season and the tension of the case...”

“What’s wrong with any of that?” she asked, her voice so husky with need, she could barely speak.

“Nothing, except—you’re going to respect me even less in the morning.” His arm went swiftly around her and his mouth came down to hers. Unable to hold back anymore, Carter decided that if he was going to be nothing more to her than a toy, something to relieve the sexual need she was surprising him with, then he was going to be the best sex toy she would ever possess.

Dear Reader,

Mothers—you have to love them. Mallory Trent not only loves her efficiency-expert mother, but faithfully follows the rules set out in Ellen Trent's bestselling books on creating perfect order in one's life and never veering from one's routines. When Mallory is pushed, kicking and screaming, into a second chance with Carter Compton, a man she's desired for years, she discovers that she'll definitely have to *veer* if she intends to make Carter see her as a woman.

She needs an image change, and fast, if she expects Santa Claus to give her Carter for Christmas. In this moment of crisis along comes none other than Maybelle Ewing from *A Long Hot Christmas,* who, as Maybelle herself would put it, "gits bored real easy" and has given up feng shui decorating to become "ImageMakers, a new you in no time flat."

But Carter's not eager to be "gotten." Tired of his "lady-killer" image, he wants Mallory to respect him as a lawyer, meaning it's important for him to treat her like one of the guys.

Does he have a chance against Maybelle's advice and Mallory's wiles? Especially when he's sharing a hotel suite with a Mallory who's a lot sexier than she was when they studied together as law students and getting sexier every day? Surrounded by mistletoe and lighted trees in the glitter of New York in the holiday season? Poor man. As I was writing *Mistletoe Over Manhattan,* the story of his futile fight against amazing womanpower, I actually began to feel a bit sorry for him.

So turn to chapter one and let the battle begin!

Happy holidays,

Barbara Daly

BARBARA DALY

MISTLETOE OVER MANHATTAN

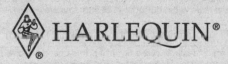

HARLEQUIN®

TORONTO • NEW YORK • LONDON
AMSTERDAM • PARIS • SYDNEY • HAMBURG
STOCKHOLM • ATHENS • TOKYO • MILAN • MADRID
PRAGUE • WARSAW • BUDAPEST • AUCKLAND

To Jennifer Green,
in celebration of our first book together.

ISBN 0-373-69153-X

MISTLETOE OVER MANHATTAN

This edition published by arrangement with Harlequin Books S.A.

Visit us at www.eHarlequin.com

Printed in U.S.A.

1

WHAT A RELIEF TO BE HOME.

Mallory Trent stepped out of the elevator on the fifty-third floor of the Hamilton Building in the Chicago Loop and gazed lovingly at the brass plaque beside the massive walnut double doors. It read Sensuous, Inc., and below that, Legal Department. After the horrible experience she'd just escaped, that plaque looked like a Welcome, Mallory sign on the pearly gates of Heaven.

The horrible experience had taken place on St. John's Island in the Caribbean. Five days on St. John's might be viewed as a vacation by some people. Some people might even have stayed the full seven days they'd originally planned to. Apparently some people enjoyed sunburn, scorpion sightings and sand grating between their toes. She wasn't one of those people. She was happier at work. Let the icy winds blow across Lake Michigan. She didn't care. She had a PalmPilot to keep her warm. She could pick up mangoes and pineapples at her local specialty market. And she had Sensuous, the cosmetics company whose offices filled the top five floors of the building and was her Heaven on earth.

"Hi, Cassie," she said to the first of her colleagues she passed in the hall.

Cassie, a smooth-skinned, pretty woman with soft, curly black hair who could open sealed boxes with her razor-sharp tongue, stared at her with wide, startled dark eyes. "You're finally back," she said in a whisper. "Bill's about to have a stroke."

"But I wasn't supposed to be back until—" Mallory said.

"Later," Cassie said, hurrying on. "Got to find out if *he's* in the building."

"Who? Bill? I imagine he's..." But she was talking to thin air, and approaching her from Cassie's direction was Ned Caldwell, another of the junior members of the legal team that provided in-house counsel to Sensuous. Ned was Cassie's opposite, a bespectacled man who spoke slowly and thought deeply. He saw her, slowed and moved toward her with an increasingly funereal expression.

"If it's serious," he murmured, "let me know how I can help."

"Help with—" But he was gone, too, scurrying away with unusual speed as if Mallory were carrying a fatal virus—which, for all she knew, she might be. A virus transmitted by squadrons of foot-long mosquitoes that traveled in formation, like the ones in St. John's. Mallory fought down an urge to go back to her apartment, take two aspirin and check in the next morning. Instead, she forged onward into her office suite and looked warily at the administrative aide whose services she shared with Cassie and Ned.

"Good morning, Hilda," she said firmly, daring the woman to say anything out of the ordinary.

"You're back!" Hilda said in a loud whisper, clasping a hand to her ample bosom. "Bill Decker wants to see you immediately."

"How does he know I'm here?" Mallory whispered back. "And why are we all whispering?"

Hilda raised her voice to a low drone. "He doesn't. On Friday he called every thirty minutes to ask if I'd located you yet, and every thirty minutes I reminded him you were on vacation, and...and...I lied!" She rolled her eyes heavenward. "I told him you'd refused to tell me how to reach you."

"Hilda!" No wonder Bill was hysterical. "He knows I'd never, never do that!"

"I just wanted you to have a vacation for once in your life—" The phone buzzed. "Oh, hell, I bet that's him again."

Hilda never swore. What was making everyone so tense?

"Yes, Mr. Decker," Hilda was saying, her calm restored by her little outburst. "She, ah, she—" Hilda darted a quizzical glance at Mallory.

Mallory nodded. "Tell him I just walked in. Two days early," she couldn't help adding. Something was out of kilter, and she couldn't deal with life when it went out of kilter.

"She'll be there shortly," Hilda said, and when she'd disconnected, she gazed up at Mallory. "I want you to know—" she was back in her whispering mode "—I'm on your side, whatever happens."

Mallory tightened her lips and squared her shoulders, picked up her PalmPilot and tugged at the hemline of her neat black suit jacket. She took a step forward, then paused to extend each leg in front of her, twisting each foot to the left and then to the right, to assure herself that the polished gleam of her sensible black pumps had not picked up a speck of dust while she had so unwisely exiled herself to the Caribbean.

An early book of her mother's had advised, "Career success depends on keeping your work wardrobe in perfect condition—your suits clean, blouses pressed, shoes shined and protected by flannel shoe bags."

Her friends hooted at Ellen Trent's literary masterpieces—how-to bestsellers that taught both housewife and career woman to achieve domestic perfection with maximum efficiency. Mallory followed them to the letter. If she were ever a witness in a court case, she'd demand to swear on a stack of her mother's books.

Her mother would be proud of her now as she strode down the hall to the office of the legal department's head honcho, Bill Decker, with the confident carriage of a nobleperson. In this case, it appeared that the nobleperson might be on her way to the guillotine, but if her head rolled, her hair would be shining with good health and sporting a recent cut. She would die with her PalmPilot in her hand and her nails perfectly manicured.

From the way her colleagues were acting, she could only infer that she'd done something terribly, disastrously wrong. Something she couldn't even guess at. Maybe she was about to be fired. For a second, that stopped her in her tracks. Of all the things in the world Mallory had imagined could happen to her—being overworked, underpaid, taken for granted, used, ignored—being fired was at the bottom of the list.

You could cruise the indices of her mother's books until the end of time and you wouldn't find a reference to "adjusting efficiently to being fired." It was unthinkable in the Trent household, equally unthinkable for one of Ellen Trent's disciples and out of the question when you qualified for both categories.

"YOU FINALLY CAME BACK." Bill Decker, who should have been thrilled to see her, frowned, just as a woman at the gym frowns when you're emerging from a shower she's been waiting for. That frown saying, "What took you so long?" instead of a smile saying, "Thanks for showering so swiftly."

"I'm back two days early." It was a point she felt she had to keep drumming into him. He had no right to expect her until Wednesday. This was Monday, the Monday after Thanksgiving, a Monday she'd intended to spend lying supine on a beach chair—until she found out how maddeningly boring, how unproductive, how *inefficient* that was. She'd even paid a hundred-dollar penalty to the airline for the privilege of coming back early. That's how badly she wanted out of that beach chair.

The impatient wave of his hand prevented her from spelling it out. "Sensuous is in deep trouble," he said. "The Green case is more than we can handle in-house. We've hired outside counsel. The law firm we're using is Rendell and Renfro, and a young litigator named—" He broke off to pick up a phone. "Nancy, is Compton in the building today?"

A cold chill crept up Mallory's spine, freezing the noncommittal smile on her face.

"Ask him to come in for a minute," Decker was saying.

Could there possibly be more than one Compton who was a trial lawyer at Rendell and Renfro?

She steeled her spine while Decker's voice rolled on, seeming to echo through the fog in her mind. "As I was saying, Carter Compton's going to handle the case. I imagine you know him. Good lawyer. Bit of a rascal, I'm told." His chuckle was annoyingly indulgent. "He's going to New York to depose the plaintiffs' witnesses. We thought it would be a good idea to have a female on his team, and of course you're the right choice. Ah. Here he is."

However steeled, frozen and otherwise numb, Mallory still wasn't prepared for Carter Compton to step through the doorway. Her heart pounded. Her mouth went dry. Her lips cracked as she managed a thin smile. It took all the energy she had to stand up.

"Mallory! Great news we're going to be working together." With a flash of white teeth, Carter stepped forward and instead of shaking her hand, threaded his fingers through hers.

Electricity shot through her at the intimacy of the touch. He was a man with presence, a powerful man, tall and muscled, and his hand was large and warm, with long, broad fingers. She could feel the single callus, the one between the first and second fingers of his right hand, where he'd always gripped a pen as if it were a cigarette, maybe still needing the feel of the cigarettes he'd given up long ago under the influence of his college football coach, he'd told her. Did he still grip that pen?

Memories of this legendary lady-killer flooded through her. They'd been in law school together, studied together, worked on the Law Review together. In fact...

That one memory she'd been blocking for years rushed to the front of her mind. Before the second semester final exams, she and Carter had once spent the night together studying in his apartment—and he hadn't made a single pass at her.

"Where've you been hanging out all this time?" he asked. "I never see you."

He was giving her a puzzled look, and she wondered how long she'd been staring at him, slack-jawed and cow-eyed. "I've been here," she said, slipping her hand out of his grasp. "Just busy."

His dark hair had been long and unruly then. For the last several years, when she'd glimpsed him at work parties—then escaped to the opposite side of the room—she'd noticed the short, crisp cut he was sporting. Was it soft to the touch, she wondered, or springy? He dressed more elegantly every year. Today he was in charcoal pinstripes and a shirt with a finely patterned tatersall check. A textured black tie and a starched white handkerchief in his breast pocket completed the polished look. He'd come a long way from the jeans and bomber jackets he'd worn as a law student.

Lord, how sexy he'd been in those hip-hugging jeans. A hot, heavy weight dropped straight down Mallory's center as the image crystallized in her mind.

What hadn't changed at all was the flashing indigo of his eyes, with their fringe of thick, dark lashes. Now, having those eyes focused on her, Mallory recognized the other thing that hadn't changed. She still lusted after him with all the sophistication of a high school sophomore in the throes of her first crush.

Heat rushed to her face when she realized she was staring again. "And I guess I'm about to be busier," she said, willing her voice to come out cool and steady. "But I'm not sure our working together is a done deal yet."

Bill laughed. "It is as far as I'm concerned. Sit down, you two. We'll firm up the plans right now."

Mallory collapsed into her chair. "I'm flattered to be asked, of course," Mallory said to Bill. "I have spent quite a bit of time on the case. Did you say we'd be taking the depositions in New York?"

If she was going to work in close proximity to Carter,

how would she manage to keep her hands off him? How could she work in a state of continuous arousal?

"Yes."

She'd get herself under control. She had to. It would be too humiliating if she came on to him and he rejected her, and vastly more humiliating if he didn't even notice she was coming on to him. Besides, she was her mother's daughter. One simply got whatever it was under control.

"When would we leave?" She'd need a little extra time to get this one under control.

"Tomorrow," Bill said.

"Oh, tomorrow." With enormous relief, Mallory saw an escape hatch. "Well, I can't do that."

Decker frowned. "Why not?"

"I just got back. You know what an in-box looks like after a few days out of the office." She darted a glance at Carter, who'd sat down at last, reducing his physical impact on the room. Unfortunately his devastatingly electrical gaze was increasing his physical impact on *her*.

"Hilda can handle your in-box. So it's settled."

"Hilda can't handle the Thornton patent case," Mallory said, desperately grasping at her last salvation. "Writing that brief is the number one priority on my to-do list. You wouldn't want me to let Product Development down." She sent another glance at Carter. He'd winged up one eyebrow, which made her heart pound.

"Patents." Decker dismissed patents with a wave of the hand. "Cassie can write the brief." Carter nodded his agreement.

Mallory counted Cassie as one of her best friends, but Cassie was highly competitive. Mallory could just imagine how thrilled she'd be to hear she'd gotten one of the dregs from the bottom of Mallory's in-box. "That wouldn't be fair to her," she said. "I said I'd..."

"Mallory." Decker's voice assumed a new level of authority.

"Yes, sir?" She swallowed hard.

"I need you in New York. Are you saying you won't go?"

"No, sir. That's not what I'm saying." She couldn't help herself. Her early training had taught her to separate the generals from the privates.

"Good," he said. "Then it's settled."

"Where do you live?" Carter said.

It was the last question she'd expected. "Ah. I, um, I live, ah..." Surely she could remember her address. Finally she managed to spit it out.

"I was thinking we could drive to O'Hare together, but I'm too far out of your way. Okay if we meet at the gate? My secretary made the reservations. Your aide can call her, take it from there."

"Gate," Mallory stammered, nodding. "Ticket."

A quick goodbye to Bill, a flashing smile in Mallory's direction and he was gone. Mallory sank back into her chair.

Bill was wearing a satisfied expression. "I knew you were the right person to do this job."

"Why?" It came out like a sigh.

He beamed at her. "You're immune to Carter Compton's manly charms. I can trust you. Anywhere. With anyone." He leaned forward, his expression shining with sincerity. "I can read a person like a book, and I saw it, just now, while you were chatting with Compton. Your colleagues think of you as a lawyer, not as a woman."

On another day Mallory might have taken Bill's backhanded compliment in stride. All he meant was that she was a trusted colleague, a woman who didn't use her sexuality to her professional advantage. But seeing Carter had set off something weird in her mind. Her fingers fumbled with the PalmPilot she usually handled with such dexterity. "High praise indeed," she mumbled through lips that felt cold and numb. "Thanks again, Bill." She stood up. "I'll be ready to leave tomorrow."

On her way back to her office she thought, *Bill saw it, too. Carter doesn't see me as a woman.*

Suddenly overheated from frustration, she quickened her step and opened the door to her office suite, where she found Hilda, Cassie and Ned waiting like circled wagons.

"What happened?" they said in chorus.

"Did he fire you?" Ned added an appropriately lugubrious expression to his thick southern drawl.

"Did you find out what *he's* doing in the building?" Cassie's interest was no longer a mystery now that Mallory knew who *he* was.

"Should I order boxes for clearing out your office?" Hilda sounded anxious.

Still feeling dazed, Mallory let her eyes drift from one to the other. "No, Hilda, you should call Carter Compton's secretary and get me a plane ticket."

She heard Cassie's gasp, but forged on.

"He's taking on the Green case. Bill has assigned me to go to New York with him to depose the plaintiffs' witnesses."

In the thunderous silence, Cassie's eyes widened while her mouth thinned out into a vicious line. "I hate you!" she yelled. "I was dying, *dying*, for that assignment." She stomped into her office, from which immediately came the sounds of objects hitting the wall.

"Pack enough condoms to last a couple of days," Ned suggested, his mild, owlish gaze swinging back from Cassie's closed door to Mallory's face. "Carter's the Casanova of the twenty-first century, a legend in his time. Are you on the Pill?"

"Keep your knees locked together," Hilda said, wincing as the crashing sounds increased in volume.

Still in slow motion, Mallory stared at Ned, then at Hilda. "But you see," she said in the calm manner of the totally shocked, "that's why Bill's sending me. Because I don't need the Pill and I won't need the condoms. My knees are already permanently locked together. I am not a woman. I am a lawyer."

She drifted into her own office and closed the door just in time to see her framed diploma from the University of Chicago School of Law jump off its hook from the impact of whatever Cassie had just thrown against the dividing wall. A thin ray of sunlight broke through the uncertain winter sky to illuminate its glass as it shattered into a million glittering shards.

It seemed significant, somehow.

Mallory opened her PalmPilot to her to-do list. "Have diploma reframed," she wrote with the slim plastic stylus.

CARTER RETURNED TO THE legal department library in a thoughtful mood. He was very glad Mallory was going with him to New York. Good old Mallory. With her on the job, he wouldn't have to spend half his time in sexual fencing: the way he'd have to with most women.

He was getting tired of it, starting to want something real, starting to think about settling down.

With Paige, maybe. Well, no, not Paige. Not for the long run. Even a long weekend was sort of a stretch.

He'd eliminated Diana last weekend.

Andrea, then. Uh-uh. He never quite connected with Andrea, never felt they were talking about the same thing.

What about Marcie? Marcie was smart and sexy, and had made no secret of the fact that she'd like their relationship to grow, blossom and produce an engagement ring set with a diamond of substantial size. He didn't know why, after he'd been with her, he sometimes felt a little—empty.

An unprecedented mood of dissatisfaction settled over him. He dated dozens of girls, and dozens more wished he'd ask them out or accept their thinly veiled invitations. One of them had to be just right.

In the meantime, he loved his work, and this was the craziest case he'd ever lucked into. Just thinking about it dispelled his bad mood. Its proper name was *Kevin Knightson et al. v. Sensuous.* Informally, they referred to it as the Green case, because last March a hundred or so women plus a few men had attempted to dye their hair Sensuous Flaming Red, and instead, had dyed their hair—and everything else the solution had touched—pea-green, as the brief described it.

They didn't think it was funny. He'd better make sure he didn't let on he thought it was funny. Mallory sure wouldn't think it was funny. He'd be able to count on her to keep his face straight.

He could count on her for everything, just as he had in law school. That time they'd studied all night—something in his head had gone *click* and he'd finally gotten it together. It had taken a lot of hard work, but that one night had turned his law school record around.

He'd been sorely tempted to end the night with Mallory in his bed, at least to hold that tall, slim woman in his arms and give her a kiss that said, "Thanks, and let's get together sometime." A kiss that would make her *want* to get together sometime.

Why hadn't he?

He'd gotten himself together was what had happened, had gotten the second highest grade on that exam. Mallory, of course, had gotten the highest.

Funny, he'd forgotten how pretty she was with her pale, blue-green eyes and that incredible silvery-blond hair.

He realized he was worrying his pen between his index and middle fingers, a nervous habit he'd been trying to break. His time was too valuable to waste it like this. He'd been thinking about the case, which was all he could afford to think about until he negotiated a settlement. Sensuous had recalled that entire lot of dye upon getting the first complaint, of course, and had sent lawyers out to negotiate generous settlements to the first fifteen or twenty of those hundred plus complainants. Unfortunately, a couple of the complainants had found an ambitious lawyer—or she had found them, which happened sometimes—who got all of them together and filed suit. They weren't going to settle for hair therapy, weekly manicures, new sinks, repainted walls and regrouted tile floors anymore. They were after everything Sensuous was worth.

And all because a bored assembly line man had decided it would be fun to add a permanent green dye to a batch of hair color in honor of St. Patrick's Day.

Carter's first priority was to keep the case from going to trial, which was one of the ironies of being a trial lawyer. He'd do his best to convince these pea-green plaintiffs that weekly manicures and new sinks were all the payback they needed.

He hoped Sensuous had hired him for his professional reputation, not his personal one. He hoped they didn't think he could seduce the plaintiffs and their lawyer—a woman—into settling.

"Mr. Compton?" He looked up to see one of the department's paralegals at the library door. "I know you have permission to access the Green case files on our network, but I made you a CD as backup in case you're somewhere without a network connection." The girl's hands trembled as she handed him the packaged disk.

"Thanks," he said, standing up, giving her a smile. For a second he was afraid she was going to faint. Then what would he do? But she mustered up some poise, returned his smile, batted her lashes and swung her hips provocatively as she made her way out of the library. At the door she paused, struck a sexy pose, gave him some more eyelash action and said, "I'm Lisa, and if there's anything else I can do to help, like if you need clerical or paralegal backup in New York..."

It was the story of his life. He couldn't help it. It wasn't anything he did deliberately. Some chemical in his body—well, testosterone was what it was—must have sprung a leak at birth and had been oozing out of him ever since, attracting women like beer attracted slugs.

If he intended to settle down, he had to plug that leak. He had to become irresistible to just one woman. And he had to stop attracting every unattached female who came into view. There was no better time than right now to give it a try. He wondered what he could say that would leave no doubt in Lisa's mind that he wouldn't be calling her for a wild weekend in New York. And while he wondered and Lisa waited, a bright idea popped into his mind.

"Thanks, Lisa," he said. "I'll pass that on to Mallory Trent. She's going to need plenty of support from the department."

He was relieved to hear the smoky tone clear from Lisa's voice. "Of course," she said, releasing her body from the arched-back position that made her breasts and butt stick out at the same time. "I'm happy to give Mallory any help she needs."

When she slammed the library door, Carter felt he'd made some progress. He'd discovered, he ruminated as he made his way back to his own handsome office at Rendell and Renfro, that it paid to have a woman on his team who could run interference for him with other women.

While they were in New York, Mallory would make a great blocker.

Of course, he didn't want to be blocked completely. On his phone list were several women who lived in New York. This was his chance to go out with them, enjoy their company, treat them to a night on the town—and if he felt like it, a night in bed. Along the way, he'd determine if one of them might be someone he could settle down with forever. He'd make dates with a couple of them right now, tonight, before he forgot.

He reached his building, signed in and went up to his office. Too bad the plaintiffs didn't have Mallory's hair. Nobody with hair like Mallory's would want to dye it red.

2

MALLORY DIDN'T OPEN her office door again until she'd heard her suitemates leave for the day. By that time she felt she'd successfully compartmentalized every facet of her life, including Carter, who'd gone into a read-only-don't-touch file. And there he would stay, at least until she had to face him in person at the airport in the morning. By morning, she'd be herself again. Under control.

Dressed for the cold winter night, she caught a cab on LaSalle, which slipped and slid as it carried her through the velvety darkness. The streetlamps cast a golden glow on the snowflakes that misted the air and iced the streets. Christmas trees soared high within the lobbies of the commercial buildings she passed, and when she reached the more residential areas, glittered festively through the windows of brownstones and apartments.

"It's beginning to look a lot like Christmas," the cab driver said.

Resisting an alarming urge to sing, "everywhere you go," back at him, Mallory said, "We just had Thanksgiving."

"That's Chicago for you. Start on Christmas and Hanukkah while we're still living on turkey leftovers."

"We are mere tools of the commercial establishment," Mallory said, sighing even as her spirits rose in anticipation of her parents' pleasure in the gifts she'd already gotten for them—a new, state-of-the-art laptop for her mother, which she'd asked her brother Macon to select and load with the most up-to-date software, and a fully accessorized riding lawnmower for her father, which would enable him to keep the lawn in Oak Park groomed to military standards.

"You got that right," her philosophical driver agreed, nodding. "No love in the presents anymore, just money."

Money. She'd spent a ton of money on those gifts. But, she argued with herself, she'd also spent a ton of time deciding what might please them most.

Still, it was something to think about, and she had plenty of time to think while the taxi driver told her a heart-wrenching story about the Christmas his great-aunt gave him a sweater she'd knitted with her own two hands, and on the day after Christmas, had passed on, leaving her memory behind in perfect cable stitch.

She gave him a generous tip when he dropped her at her high-rise in the Carl Sandburg Village in Old Town. When she stepped through the door, she found her apartment, as always, silent, warm, spotless and perfectly neat, just as it should be and would be, unless she drifted unknowingly into senility—still living in this apartment.

A grim resignation came over her as that thought went through her mind, but this wasn't the time to attack and disarm it. She put her black leather briefcase on the desk in her home office off the kitchen, lining it up precisely beside the desk pad. Today's mail went beneath the mail that had arrived while she was stoically enduring her vacation. First in, first out. That was the rule.

Go through mail.

Pay bills. Respond to invitations and requests.

Read and throw away or file everything else.

This list, an excerpt from one of her mother's books, popped into her mind. No wonder the surprise encounter with Carter had thrown her completely off balance. She'd gotten in too late the night before—and had been too traumatized by warmth, sand and the mandate to relax—to follow her customary mail routine. A happy life, her mother asserted in every book, was a series of learned habits, or routines. And if you ever veered from one of your routines, it was the first step toward a downward slide into chaos and misery.

As always, her mother was right. She'd veered, her mental state was in chaos and she was miserable. So the mail would be her top priority after she finished her homecoming routine. No more veering.

As she slid a black leather glove into each pocket of her black cashmere coat, her gaze fell to the rectangular box on top of the stack. It was a complimentary copy of the latest Ellen Trent book. Just what she needed at the moment—a quick refresher course.

She hung the coat in the foyer closet, her black cashmere scarf tucked under the collar, and centered her black hat on the shelf directly above it. With her snow boots drying in a special snow-boot box just outside the front door of the apartment, she carried the black flannel bag that held her still-gleaming Soft 'N' Comfy pumps to her bedroom.

The pumps were black, too, as were the snow boots. Why didn't she have anything—red?

It's always best to stick to basic black in cold-weather climates and beige for warmer environments.

Another quote from a book of her mother's. That explained it. It didn't explain a peculiar knot of rebellion that rolled through Mallory from her scalp to her toes. She did have something red. Wine. She went straight to the kitchen and poured herself a glass, then went back to the office to start her mail routine.

She swished the wine around in the glass, admiring its color and examining its rim, sniffed it, analyzing its bouquet, then took a totally undiscriminating gulp. The warmth cascaded down her throat, startling her into staring at the glass in her hand, unable to imagine how it had gotten there. Wine and paperwork didn't go together. Everybody knew that, at least everybody who preferred a balanced checkbook. See what she'd done? She'd veered again! What was wrong with her, anyway? Nothing a dose of her mother's wisdom couldn't cure. She ripped open the box that held the new book.

Efficient Travel From A to Z was its predictable title, and clipped to the front was a sheet of notepaper with her mother's letterhead. The message was typed: Compliments of Ellen Trent.

None too warm and motherly. Inside was a letter, also typed, but a little more warm and motherly.

Dearest daughter:
This one's a compilation of all my travel tips plus a few exciting new ideas! Hope they help you remember Ellen's Golden Rule: Efficiency is the key to a happy life.
Mother

Not finding a hug anywhere in the message, unless "dearest" was meant to be one, Mallory scanned the table of contents: "Beauty in a Baggie," "Carry On,"

"Delete, That's the Key"—these chapter titles sounded familiar and had probably appeared as articles in women's magazines. But "Returning to Serenity," which cleverly filled two alphabet slots, was new. Mallory opened to that chapter.

Leave your paperwork in order.

That was already tops on Mallory's to-do list.

Don't leave any dirty laundry behind.

Well, of course not. Her dry cleaner opened at seven. She'd drop off her resort clothes on the way to the plane tomorrow morning. The dry cleaner would charge an exhorbitant rate for washing and pressing her clothes, but she didn't have time to do laundry in the basement of the apartment building, and rules were rules.

Clean your refrigerator thoroughly, and pay special attention to the crisper. A rotten vegetable will spoil your return to hearth and home.

No problem there. She hadn't been home long enough to put anything in the crisper.

Check the expiration date of your perishables—boxed, canned, frozen and refrigerated foods and over-the-counter drugs—and throw away those items that will expire while you're away.

Mallory stared at the page, briefly considering the possibility that her mother had at long last gone over the edge. But millions of women bought these books, women who pursued the same kind of happiness her mother enjoyed, that Mallory relied upon and took comfort from.

Give your itinerary to a close friend or family member.

This brought her up short. If she called her parents, the conversation would take hours. Her mother would put her through a verbal checklist, and they might get into a fight over the expiration date thing. She had friends. Close friends. The friends with whom she'd taken the St. John's trip, for example, who'd stared at her in disbelief when she'd announced her intention to come home early. They'd tease her mercilessly if she told them she'd traded sun and sand for sin and sex with Carter Compton.

Her head jolted up from the book with a snap that almost left her with whiplash. She was going to New York on business, not to engage in sin and sex.

She suddenly remembered she had a brother in New York she could send her itinerary.

It wasn't surprising she was just now remembering that Macon was in New York. Macon was the sort of person whose location was vague, not so much a brother as a cyber-brother. He communicated with the family by e-mail. He sent Internet birthday cards and gifts he'd ordered online. Occasionally he came home for Christmas, but more often, he spent the holiday monitoring some public or private computer system. Macon was a computer ace. He lived and breathed computers, had since he met a keyboard and experienced love at first byte.

From time to time, their parents took a notion to make sure he still existed in the flesh. After their last trip to New York, Mallory's mother had reported that he was dressing better these days. But then, it was hard to believe he could be dressing any worse.

She dialed his number. Predictably, the phone rang once and a message came on. "Trent Computer Consultants," Macon's familiar voice droned. "I'm not here. E-mail me at macontrent, all one word, at trent dot com."

"My brother the robot," Mallory muttered.

Whose sister isn't a woman, she's a lawyer.

The similarity was too great. Getting up from the computer after e-mailing Macon to tell him they should get together in New York, she felt exhausted. She'd better pack before she found herself checking the expiration dates on the box of crackers and tin of smoked oysters she kept on hand as an emergency hors d'oeuvre. She turned to the chapter entitled "Carry On." She didn't really need to look at it. This chapter she knew by heart.

CARTER COMPTON WRAPPED his fingers around his most recent cup of coffee, took a sip and made a face. It was the worst coffee he'd ever tasted—okay, except for the last cup he'd made for himself. He'd had to resort to the vending machine in the basement, since the staff in the firm's lounge had gone home hours ago.

He put down the cup and picked up his pen, flipping it back and forth between his fingers. He figured if he worked until nine, he could pick up a pizza on the way home, eat it while he packed and be in bed by ten. His secretary had ordered a car service to pick him up at six-thirty in the morning. That left no time to think. Just the way he liked it.

Something had caused an atmospheric disturbance today. He'd thought his atmosphere had become as dependable as the sunrise and no longer vulnerable to disturbance. Not being able to pin down what had caused it was more disturbing than the disturbance itself.

He had a feeling it was something about Mallory.

The Sensuous files on the Green case had occupied him for several hours. Mallory being all business, she'd probably want to discuss the case during the flight, and he wanted to sound as if he'd given it some thought.

His life was crawling with women, and here he was, trying to impress Mallory. He guessed he'd never feel secure enough about his professional expertise to get over the early days, when he'd had to pull out all the stops to change people's impression of him.

He got up, stepped over to the big windows of his office and looked out at the glitter of Chicago. Christmas lights already. In the posh suburb of Kenilworth where he'd grown up, his parents had always had the biggest, most beautiful florist-decorated Christmas tree in the neighborhood, if you could call a tree that had a recognizable theme a Christmas tree, and if you could call the collection of huge houses on large acreages a neighborhood. Under that tree were mountains of presents, everything he wanted plus things he didn't know he wanted. And, always, a tiny box from his father to his mother, containing a diamond slightly larger than the diamond he'd given her the year before.

He'd been a spoiled rich kid, an only child who didn't know the meaning of rules. With every advantage life could offer, instead of making the most of them, he'd run wild. He'd lost his driver's license twice for speeding, had totaled three sports cars—somehow, he couldn't imagine how—without hurting anybody. He'd done enough damage to end up getting accused of things he hadn't done. His parents had had to post bail for him when he was arrested for burglarizing a neighboring house. He hadn't, but he couldn't blame the police for suspecting him. Stealing and drugs were about the only two things he hadn't experimented with.

Oh, yes. He'd never gotten a girl pregnant, which he

saw as something of a miracle—the miracle being that his father had deposited a huge box of condoms on his dresser every Friday morning.

Good grades would only have ruined his high school reputation. He'd played football, but the coach was a diplomat used to dealing with the rich parents of spoiled rich kids, and as long as the team made a decent showing, he didn't impose many rules, either.

So Carter had managed to get into Northwestern University in Evanston by playing football. There the coach had made him quit smoking, drinking, eating junk food and staying up all night with the cheerleader of his choice to prepare himself for the game the next day. But nobody found out how smart he was until he took the LSATs before applying to law school.

One look at his scores, and the University of Chicago Law School had snapped him up. What they didn't know was that he didn't know how to study, and that's where Mallory had turned his life around. He couldn't remember exactly how it had happened, just that he'd called her, admitted he was floundering and asked for her help. And she'd been his unofficial, unpaid tutor. He'd never even taken her out for dinner. He'd been afraid to ask.

Did she remember what a dolt he'd been?

Carter frowned. He'd better do a little more work, get familiar with the details, have a few intelligent questions to ask Mallory and, even better, a couple of intelligent comments to make. In short, he'd better get off this nostalgia trip and focus on the damned files.

THE PHONE RANG JUST as Mallory finished packing the flexible wardrobe her mother had been claiming for years would get a woman through anything for any length of time. True to form, when she finished, she actually had room to spare.

"Mallory? Carter," said the caller.

It was like a tummy punch, that deep, warm voice. "Hi, Carter." She kept hers cool as a waterfall. That was just how great an impact her mother's books had on her. A short session with that practical, unromantic voice had returned her to her normal, sane self. She would be fine on this trip.

"I'm calling with a question," he said. "Why pea-green? Why not just green?"

Mallory blinked. "Well—" She was confident there was a reason, but the sound of his voice, the very fact that he'd called, was making inroads on her normal, sane self. It was maddening. "There are numerous shades of green, lime-green, forest-green, Kelly-green..."

"Would you be less upset if your hair were lime-green instead of pea-green?"

"Um. No, I suppose not."

"Then the use of 'pea-green,' which has a negative connotation, instead of just 'green,' which is more neutral, is a deliberate attempt on the part of the plaintiffs to make the green sound as disgusting as possible." He sounded triumphant.

"But I just said it wouldn't matter if—"

"Just something to think about. Okay. See you at the gate tomorrow."

"Okay, I'll—" But he wasn't there anymore. It was the first time he'd called her since law school, and all he'd wanted was to discuss the impact of pea-green over plain green on a potential jury.

She whirled to stare at herself in the mirror. She might not be gorgeous, but why, exactly, didn't her colleagues think of her as a woman? Forget the colleagues. Why hadn't Carter ever seen her as a woman?

She had to admit she looked none too sexy with her teeth clenched together. She whirled back, and her gaze fell on her suitcase. She still had room. What could she take that was a little more exciting than black and more black and a touch of white?

With frantic fingertips she went through the sparse collection of clothes in her closet, wondering why she bothered. She knew what she owned. More black, more white, a small navy grouping and the thrill of one gray suit and one beige. No surprises were hiding in there.

It was too late to go shopping, but not too late to call her friend Carol the Consummate Clotheshorse down on the fifth floor. Carol had flown back early from St. John's, too, for a reason their friends understood, to make a raid on Marshall Field's post-Thanksgiving, pre-Christmas sales racks. She'd have something old she'd be willing to loan.

"Carol," she began, "I'm going to New York."

"Mallory the Jet-setter," Carol said. "Didn't know you had it in you."

Mallory clenched her teeth. "It's business," she said crisply. "I was wondering if I might borrow one extra jacket from you."

"Anything," Carol said fervently. "If you'd wear something besides a suit and midheel orthopedic pumps, I'd give you rights to my whole closet. All my closets," she corrected herself. "What kind of jacket did you have in mind?"

"Something that goes well with black," Mallory said, floundering in the alternatives and also realizing this wasn't the first time a friend had commented on her penchant for suits and dowdy shoes. It was just the first time it had upset her.

A dangerous thought ran through her mind. Herself in a low-necked, scarlet top, and Carter's fingertips edging the cleavage, then dipping beneath the fabric...

She stammered the words out. "I was thinking...red." There. She'd veered again. It was getting easier each time. Not processing her mail, then wine, now red.

"Ooh," Carol said. "I've got a red jacket that would look great on you. I'll bring it right up and hang it on your doorknob. I know you're busy packing."

Mallory was already having second thoughts, but a red jacket seemed like such a tiny veer that it hardly seemed worth worrying about. "Thanks, Carol. I'll return the favor as soon as possible."

"You can return it right now. Do you have any stamps?"

"Of course." She had every staple of everyday life in bulk, just as the efficient woman should. "I'll leave them on the foyer table. And Carol?"

"Um?"

"May I leave you a copy of my itinerary?"

"Sure. But you said New York. Just tell me where you're staying."

"The St. Regis," Mallory said, "but there's more information than that. Flight numbers, who to call just in case...."

"And the suit you'd like to be buried in," Carol said with a sigh Mallory had also heard from more than one of her friends. "I'll wait fifteen minutes before I bring up the jacket." She paused, and when she spoke again, her voice had taken on a new tone. "You're going to love this jacket."

Did Carol's voice have a sly edge, or was she imagining it? She hadn't been imagining it, a fact she learned when she unhooked the red jacket from her doorknob.

Mallory looked it over, and then, dismayed, tried it on. Had she gained weight? She and Carol had always been the same size. But this jacket hugged her waist, pushed up her breasts and flared out over her hipbones, ending much too soon to hide her rear end, which Mallory felt was the best reason to wear a jacket.

Carol had undoubtedly meant well, but Mallory was sure she could never bring herself to go out in public in this jacket. Still, she didn't want to appear ungrateful. She folded it in the "Ellen Trent fold" and used it to fill the empty space in her roll-on bag. If this insane craving for red lasted, she'd buy a proper blazer in New York.

She closed her mother's book and held it in her hand for a moment, then slid it into her suitcase. Having it with her would be like wearing garlic to ward off illness or holding a cross to shield herself from the devil.

The devil being Carter.

CARTER DRUMMED ON HIS desktop with the pen he held the same way he used to hold a cigarette. He'd thought the pea-green query had been a good question for Mallory, but he could tell from her hesitation that she'd thought it was a damned silly question and she would probably have said so if she weren't such a well-brought-up girl.

She wasn't a girl anymore. She was all woman.

Feeling as if he'd regressed ten years, he threw everything into his briefcase and went home to his Lake Shore Drive apartment. It was a mess. He was glad to be leaving it, and his cleaning service would deal with it before he got back. He'd forgotten to pick up the pizza and had to order one in. It didn't arrive until he'd finished packing, so he ate it in bed while he watched the news. He reflected that he still had that spoiled rich kid inside him, and every now and then, he had to let him out.

Feeling that the smell of pepperoni might follow him all the days of his life, he picked a thread of mozzarella cheese off his favorite pillow, pounded it into a comfortable configuration and tried very hard to get a good night's sleep.

Good luck. But exhaustion took over, and next thing he knew, he was at the airport waiting for Mallory.

So where the hell was she?

He'd arrived at the gate at a time he thought was a polite compromise between the airline's ridiculous demands and the reality of the situation, but he'd been there fifteen minutes now with no sign of the woman.

Maybe she was there and ignoring him, the way she did at work parties where he'd caught an occasional glimpse of her but could never seem to catch up with her.

With more relief than he wanted to admit to, he saw her aiming toward him, tall, elegant, dressed all in black with that silver-blond hair swinging forward on her shoulders.

As far as he knew, it was her natural hair color, and he assumed that as she grew older, it would go gently from silver-blond to silver gray. You would hardly notice. Especially since you hardly noticed Mallory in the first place.

He stood up, started to smile at her, then felt his eyebrows drawing together in a frown as he wondered why his heart had speeded up a little. He really had to cut down on the caffeine. He had so much adrenaline pumping through him all the time he didn't need caffeine at all.

She was, in fact, a great-looking woman. The man across from him was giving her an appreciative gaze as she moved between them, pulling a roll-on briefcase behind her.

Damn. She'd checked her luggage. Collecting it would take an extra thirty minutes at LaGuardia. His frown deepened, but whether it was because of the luggage or the appreciative male he was suddenly unsure.

"Hi," was all she said.

The word came through full lips of the palest pink, and her voice was rich and throaty. Something about it, or maybe it was the look that man across from him was giving her, made him put his arm around her, nothing more than a cocktail party-type hug, but his heart did an even more violent flip-flop. This was absurd. He removed his arm in a hurry and said, "Mallory. What kept you?"

He was thinking about talking to his doctor about that little aortic thing when she said, "You're here so early! How can you work here? You must be able to focus better than I can. I always wait until the very last second to get to the gate, because..."

As the appreciative man finally dropped his gaze to his newspaper, Carter had a cooling memory of the reason he hadn't tried to make love to her during their law school years. It was clear she didn't want him to. Although her voice sounded a little breathless, it was probably from hurrying, because everything else about her said, "Don't touch."

"I just got here myself," he said, and this time he managed a smile. "I guess you got held up checking bags."

"No," Mallory assured him. "This is it." She gestured toward the roll-on, and her ice-pale hair swung forward on her shoulders in a perfect, shining arc.

Carter gazed at the bag with new curiosity. What did she have in there, freeze-dried outfits that expanded when dipped in water? He'd taken Diana to Acapulco last weekend—Diana and four matched pieces of tapestry-covered luggage—where he'd discovered that looking at beautifully dressed Diana was all he would ever care to do. A wasted weekend, and he had so few free ones.

"Planning a shopping spree?" he asked Mallory.

With a single glance through blue-green eyes as ice-pale as her hair and lipstick, she made him feel like the worst and most odious of male chauvinists. "Of course not. I'm going to New York to work, not shop."

Was she always that way? Or just with him? That made her the only woman in the world who was like that with him.

"Welcome to United Airlines flight four-oh-three," an agent piped up. "We are now boarding First Class and Premier members."

Carter chewed on his lower lip while they joined the line to board. He was afraid he knew why Mallory acted this way with him, and it didn't bode well for their working relationship, which, he could easily see, was the only kind of relationship she cared to have with him.

But with so many other women in the world, why should he care?

3

AS SOON AS THEY were settled on the plane, she was going to let herself breathe. As soon as they were settled side by side in the generous first-class seats, she began to fear she might never breathe again.

One little hug and the lectures she'd given herself the night before had flown from her mind. All these years she'd done the right thing to hide on the other side of the room when she glimpsed him at professional meetings. At a cocktail party he might have kissed her! The kiss wouldn't have been any more passionate than the hug had been, but her libido didn't seem to care what state his was in. One kiss and she would have poured herself over him like a spilled Cosmopolitan. That first touch of his hand had brought back all the young, yearning feelings in full force—way too full, way too forceful.

His eyes, so darkly blue they were almost black, still advertised the passion in his body and soul—a passion for women, for life, for the law. Those eyes, and the expressive brows above them, were the key to his magnetism. Without those eyes he'd be a mere mortal—a tall, magnificently built mortal whose hair commanded you to touch it. If possible, while sitting on his lap. Straddling him. A heavy ache settled between her thighs. Not possible. Never would be possible, because...

"Something to drink before takeoff, sir?" asked the flight attendant. Her liquid hazel eyes slid smoothly over the entire and considerable length of Carter.

"Mallory?" Carter turned his gaze on Mallory rather than on the flight attendant with the roaming eyes.

"Hemlock." It came out like a soft moan. Carter and the flight attendant both stared at her. "Hazelnut," she said hastily. "Hazelnut coffee if you have it."

"No hazelnut," said the attendant.

"Plain is fine," Mallory conceded. "Decaffeinated." She couldn't take another jolt. Of anything.

"Orange juice," Carter said after a brief pause. "No, make it tomato."

You can make it with this tomato anytime, the attendant's eyes answered back.

Mallory spied on Carter out of the corner of her eye, waiting to see his flashing smile, his unspoken promise that he found the woman beautiful, and if things worked out, well, maybe. There it was, the start of a smile, followed amazingly by a frown.

That was new, Carter frowning at a flirtatious woman. And it didn't bear thinking about, because it might get her hopes up, and she had no hope of having a personal relationship with Carter. She'd just have to be content with relating to him in the one area in which she felt secure—the Green case.

"Could we use the flight time to talk about the case?" she asked him, knowing she sounded prim and stodgy next to the sexpot in uniform. "I'll boot up my laptop as soon as we're in the air so we can refer to the interrogatories."

"Oh, sure," Carter said, "the sooner we get to work the better."

Truer words had never been spoken, he thought. The plane took off smoothly, but he felt as if he'd been sucked into a tornado funnel. He only hoped the funnel would drop him somewhere safe. He had an odd feeling he wasn't safe with Mallory anymore.

He sneaked a sidelong glance at her. It wasn't her clothes. Her pantsuit looked like a good one, but it was definitely a working suit, prim and proper. Wasn't her makeup, either, even though at Sensuous, he suspected, makeup samples were among the perks of the job. Not that he knew much about makeup, but it looked as if all she'd done was darken her brows and lashes a little, put a smudge of powder on her nose and the shiny pink lipstick on her mouth and let it go at that.

They were long. Her eyelashes. He'd never noticed before. She hadn't darkened them in law school, or he hadn't been looking at anything but her grade point average. She'd gotten him through Constitutional Law, that was for sure. But now he couldn't imagine how she'd done it without his noticing her eyelashes.

"Do you think that's an approach we could use? I know it's a little unorthodox, but it might work in this particular case."

What the hell had she been saying while he was admiring her eyelashes? "Ah...um...I'll have to think it over," Carter said, tumbling out of the tornado cloud into extremely dangerous territory.

Directly onto solid ice, in fact. The ice of her blue eyes as she glared at him. "You weren't listening."

"Mallory, Mallory." He assumed the hurt, bassett hound look that had always worked when he was supposed to be romancing a woman and was instead thinking about a case. Except this time it was the other way around. "When have I ever not listened to you?"

"Just now," Mallory said, looking at him as if he were a bit of dog poop on her sturdy, sensible-looking black pump.

He guessed she'd never forget that without her help, he would have failed that Con Law exam and probably flunked out of law school. The night he studied with her had started him off on the road to respectability, but she would never be able to respect his intellect. That's why she'd never come on to him. Mallory would have to respect a man in order to feel an attraction to him

Well, he'd just have to do something to change her image of him. He also knew it would take time to win her over. For now, he would do the only thing that seemed appropriate.

He smiled at her.

ONE MINUTE SHE'D been flying on a horizontal line high above the clouds, and the next minute, transported by his smile, she was rocketing toward outer space. That smile said "woman," not "lawyer." The oddest little sensation started up in the region of her abdomen—well, lower than that—and buzzed out in all directions. Her body felt hot, damp and twitchy, while her mouth went dry.

It had also fallen open. She snapped it shut, then opened it again. "What I was suggesting was a touch of irony in the proceedings," she said from her position high above the clouds. Her voice sounded thin and high to her own ears, probably due to the lack of oxygen. "As in, 'What's so bad about pea-green hair and nails? Teenagers are paying big bucks to have green hair.'"

That smile of his widened. While it was a little less suggestive now that it was wider, it only increased its effect on her. The newspaper report flashed through her head:

Lawyer Assaults Colleague On Cross-Continental Flight

"I don't know what came over me," said Mallory Trent in her confession to the airline security squad. "I must have experienced a moment of insanity to have done something so out-of-character as to rip off my stockings and panties and fling myself on top of the plaintiff."

"You must have apprehended the wrong person," stated her immediate superior, William Decker, who heads up the legal staff of Sensuous. "It's unthinkable that Ms. Trent would behave in such a provocative way. She's not a woman, she's a—"

"That'd be an original line of defense," Carter was saying. His voice seemed to have deepened and softened. It sounded like the purr of a Rolls-Royce engine. "I'd say, 'Green hair takes thirty years off your age, madam.'"

"Then you flash her that drop-dead smile and we win the case."

She was distressed to see his smile fade, his lips tighten. For a minute she'd thought she'd stirred up a man-woman reaction in him at last, but then somehow she'd turned it off as fast as you could unplug an electric mixer. What on earth had she said?

THERE IT WAS, his first clue that he'd been assigned to this case for his people skills, not his professional ones. *No, damn it, I'm not doing it that way. I present an irrefutable argument and we win the case. Better yet, I crush the plaintiffs' testimony to dust and they beg for a settlement instead of a trial.*

Carter couldn't imagine why he was letting her get to him like this. He'd graduated fourth in their class. Rendell and Renfro was a prestigious firm. He'd already made partner, the youngest partner they'd made in years. He didn't need a—what had she called it? A drop-dead smile?—to do a good job representing Sensuous. Why couldn't she admit it?

She was tapping away on her laptop, so he let his gaze fix on her face. She was undeniably beautiful. Undeniably smart. But that didn't make him inferior. Two people could be smart at the same time.

Gazing at her, Carter made a vow. He could have sex with a host of women. What he wanted from this woman was her respect, and he'd get it while they worked on this case together, whatever the cost.

"IF YOU'LL HANDLE the cab fare and the porter, I'll check us in," Carter said when they pulled up in front of the St. Regis Hotel. The flight had seemed endless. The sooner he and Mallory were in separate rooms, the better. Leaving her whipping out bills and demanding receipts, he strode into the magnificent hotel lobby and approached the reception desk.

"Compton and Trent," he said to the navy suited woman who greeted him.

"Yes, Mr. Compton," she said after she'd punched her computer keyboard enough times to have turned out a short story for her efforts. "We have a very nice suite for you." She eyed him as all women did—speculatively.

Carter responded with a credit card. "And for Ms. Trent?"

The woman's fingers slowed. Her confidence seemed to ebb. "You and she are sharing the suite," she said at last. "The person who made the reservation said—"

Too late, Carter remembered what he'd told Brenda. "It's just Mallory," he'd said. "Do whatever sounds most convenient."

Deeply regretting that statement, he leaned across the desk. "I've changed my mind," he hissed, glancing behind him to see Mallory approaching. "Give her the suite and find another room for me."

"Aw. Did you two break up on the plane?" The clerk brightened.

His lips tightened. "No. We're professional colleagues. I just think we'd rather have some privacy after working together all day." Besides, Mallory suddenly struck him as way too cute with her forehead wrinkled up the way it was right now.

A lot more clicking of the keyboard followed. "I'm sorry, Mr. Compton," the woman finally said, "but we're fully booked this week. It's the convention, you know. Hundreds of delegates in town."

"What convention?" Carter barked. He'd steal a room from a drunk conventioneer who'd be too sloshed to notice.

"National Rifle Association," she said, looking up from the keyboard.

"Oh."

Mallory appeared beside him, looking less like a harried traveler with a lot on her mind but just as cute. "Do I need to sign for my room?" she said.

"My secretary booked us a suite," Carter said, deciding to brazen it out. "Separate rooms and baths with a sitting room we can use as an office. Sound okay to you?"

She blanched, and he knew it wasn't okay. He stiffened his spine and waited to be blasted straight through the plate-glass windows.

IT'S NOT OKAY AT ALL. But not for the reasons he was probably imagining. She'd thought the worst was over, that in a short time she'd be ensconced in her own room with her laptop up and running and no earthly need to torture herself with the sight of Carter until tomorrow. She'd skip lunch, spend the afternoon working, take a long, cool shower, order dinner from room service, snuggle up in her weightless travel robe that folded into its own pocket and spend the evening in splendid solitude. By morning, she'd have herself pulled together.

What if he suggested they have dinner?

What if he smiled at her when he suggested it?

Her knees almost buckled.

"You all right?" Carter said.

"Just fine," she lied. All she needed was time alone to gird her loins for the next day.

She wished the word *loins* hadn't come to mind. Hers were aching, and girding wasn't what they were aching for. She'd probably stay awake all night wondering if he snored. She wouldn't mind if he snored. She'd love to sleep wrapped in his arms with a soft snore vibrating against her hair. Or her throat. Or whatever his head was resting on at the moment. But not on her travel-garb-catalog wash-and-wear gown. On something silk. On naked skin.

Her head spun. She was going crazy.

She couldn't go crazy. Trents coped; they did not go crazy. What in the world was wrong with her?

She counted to ten really, really fast. "I'm fine and the room arrangement is fine," she said smoothly. "It will be convenient for working late on the case."

"It'll be just like being back in law school, studying together all night," Carter said.

With a sinking feeling, she realized how desperately she didn't want it to be anything like those nights of all work and no play.

"Here are your keys," said the clerk. "The porter will be up with your bags in a minute."

"HONEYMOONERS?" THE porter asked, settling Carter's bag on a luggage rack in one of the bedrooms of a suite that was probably larger than most New York apartments. He winked at Carter.

"Professional colleagues," Carter growled, flexing his biceps. He leaned toward the man. "Legal counsel to the National Rifle Association," he improvised.

"Oh, sorry," the porter said hurriedly. "Um, I'll show you around the place. Now here you have your thermostat..."

At that moment Mallory stepped out of her room to put her laptop down on a desk in the living area. She'd shed her jacket and was wearing a sleeveless black top tucked into her black trousers. The trousers were loose and pleated, but they fit her just great, Carter thought unexpectedly. And she had really pretty arms. Touchable arms. Arms to slide your hands up and down.

Carter noticed that the porter was looking at Mallory, too, and his spiel had trailed off. He whipped his gaze away from Mallory and onto the man again.

"And," the porter squeaked, "here you have your kitchen."

His voice warbled on. Carter actually looked at the place. He'd expected a living room in the middle and a bedroom on each side, a standard suite. Instead, there were hallways, arches and hidden entrances.

The porter, who had been in the small kitchen nervously flicking switches off and on, reappeared in the living room babbling, "...laundry service and shoeshine service. Just put your shoes outside the door at night and they'll be there in the morning, all shined up. Fitness center's in the basement. Business center's on the second floor..."

The suite was decorated in flowered stuff and velvet and Oriental rugs and crystal chandeliers. It was a home away from home—not as big as his home, but a hell of a lot neater without his stuff scattered all over it.

He was going to be shut up in here for a whole lot of nights with a woman he'd just discovered was a lot prettier and a lot sexier than he'd remembered. The stab of heat that inflamed his groin startled him. Respect was what he wanted from Mallory, and he sure wasn't going to get it if he tried to jump her bones.

"...room service twenty-four hours a day," the porter finished up. "Never have to leave the place if you don't want to."

At Carter's sharp look, he said, "But of course you'll want to, and the St. Regis offers the finest dining in New York. There's the five-star restaurant on the..."

Carter whipped out a bill and thrust it toward him.

"Oh, no need, sir," the man said, wiping sweat off

his forehead. "It was my pleasure. May I get you some ice? Extra towels?"

Carter tucked the bill in the porter's breast pocket. "Leaving would be a good idea," he said.

With numerous muttered "yessirs" the man backed out of the room.

"What did you do to that poor man?" Mallory said, sticking her head out the door of her room.

"I threatened to shoot him with an unregistered gun," Carter said.

"What?"

"Nothing. Just kidding." He dusted his hands together. "Want some lunch?"

"No, thank you. I filled up on the plane." She looked thoughtful. "It wasn't good, but it was enough."

"Yeah..." He was feeling thoughtful, too. "You won't mind having dinner alone, will you? I made some dates, women I've known for a while, thought they'd be hurt if I didn't give them a call. Athena tonight and Brie tomorrow night for starters."

"And Calpurnia Thursday night? What's your plan, to start with *A* and work through the alphabet?" She made herself smile as if she were teasing.

His face reddened. "Um, yes."

"Maybe we'll settle before you get to Zelda." She might have known. Carter would spend his days working hard, but at night he'd be messing around with women named Athena and Brie. Had she actually been hoping he'd ask her to have dinner with him? Otherwise, where did this stab of disappointment come from? "Of course I don't mind," she lied. "This arrangement mustn't make either of us feel we have to spend any time together socially."

"I didn't mean...I mean...I didn't..."

"In fact, I have plans tonight, too," she said. *While you cavort with Athena, I'll have weird food with my weird brother.* The last time she saw Macon, he'd been into Tibetan cuisine. He'd read about it on the Internet.

"You're going out?"

"Yes. And I'll be going out other nights, too. So don't think I'm going to cramp your style. We're here to work together," she summed up.

It seemed to stop him cold, which was fine with her, because she'd gone cold all over with a sudden sense of purpose that was building up inside her and had nothing whatever to do with the Green case.

She spun on one heel and went back into her room. Dialing Macon's number netted her the same advice she'd gotten from his message the night before—send him an e-mail. Muttering under her breath, she opened her door, and as Carter was apparently in his room unpacking, she retrieved her laptop from the desk, plugged it into the phone line in her room and opened her e-mail.

Sure enough, there was a message from Macon: "dear mallory i'm not in new york right now i'm in pennsylvania sorry we'll get together another time," it said.

No caps, no punctuation and he didn't sign it. He didn't feel a need to sign an e-mail when his entire name was in his address.

So Macon wouldn't be around to provide her with a reason for going out at night, or a means to compete with Carter for the "Most Active Nightlife" award. She stabbed at the reply key. "Dearest and only brother Macon: Where in Pennsylvania? What are you doing in Pennsylvania? Has it ever occurred to you that the country might use up its entire energy supply and without electricity you would simply vanish from our lives? Our cherished son and brother, lost in cyberspace. We would miss your e-mails, Macon, we truly would. Much love, your sister Mallory."

It would make him crazy—if he even saw the irony. She was in the middle of a deep sigh when Carter's voice boomed out of nowhere. "Mallory!" he shouted through her closed door.

"What!"

"I forgot to pack any socks."

She stared at the door for a minute. "I don't knit."

She heard a sound not unlike the snort of a bull as he paws the soil of the ring. Tough. If he'd read her mother's books he wouldn't have forgotten socks. She'd lend him her autographed copy.

"This is your excuse to do the loafers-no-socks thing. Of course—" she looked out the window at the bleak, gray day, at the smattering of snowflakes whitening the air, then opened the door so they wouldn't have to keep yelling at each other "—you might get frostbite and your toes would turn black and fall off. But that would cut down on your shoe size, although walking without toes might feel really odd—"

"I'm going up to Bloomingdale's to buy socks." His mouth already looked frostbitten. "I was just wondering if you'd forgotten anything and wanted to go with me."

It was her turn to be stopped cold, but she wasn't cold, she was a little bit too warm all of a sudden. "Oh. Thanks. I—" *Of course I haven't forgotten anything. I never forget anything. When you've made a proper list...* "Sure," she said. "I'll come along. I might find a Christmas present or two in the men's department." *A present a day keeps the panic away.*

No longer simply warm, she was burning up. Actually panting. Carter had asked her out.

He asked you to go to Bloomingdale's. Chill.

For the first time, it occurred to her that she was no less socially impaired than her brother was. Must have been some influence from their childhood. On the other hand, they had a handle on organization and efficiency few people could claim to have. Except that she was beginning to wonder if it was anything to boast about.

FIFTEEN MINUTES LATER Carter was randomly collecting socks from the sizeable collection in Bloomingdale's Men's First Floor Shop. Calf-length wool, patterned, whatever seemed to strike his fancy. Not a thought to matching socks which could be paired up later as they began to wear out. Mallory kept an eye on him while she chose between a black cashmere turtleneck sweater and a beige V-necked for Macon.

When she glanced back at Carter, he had built a wobbly tower of socks near the cash register. She couldn't stand it anymore. To give herself a legitimate reason to go to the cash register herself, she grabbed a sweater without looking at it and scurried over to plead her case.

"Carter?"

"Hmm? Seven, eight, nine..."

"Will that be all, miss?" A nattily dressed young clerk materialized and took the sweater from her grasp.

"Yes. Thanks," she said absently, and slid her single credit card out of its special slot in her handbag.

"Carter," she said again, "if I may make a suggestion, you really only need one more pair." As he wrestled for control of his sock pile, she imagined him saying, "Gosh, I never thought of that," and his smile would warm as he saw her in a whole new light—a womanly caretaker.

Socks clenched in his fist, he paused, turned, gazed at her. His smile didn't warm, though, and the salesman who was helping him looked positively venomous when *he* looked at her, "As I see it, I need a dozen."

"No, you don't, not if you wash out a pair every night."

His gaze intensified and his words slowed. "Why would I want to do that?"

"Because it's—" She floundered. "It's more efficient. You won't have to take all those socks back in your suitcase. You won't have to store all those extra socks at home. And if you'd buy matching socks, you could make up new pairs when one sock gets a hole in it."

"But I'd have to wash socks every night." He seemed closer to her than he had been a second ago, and the words were puffs of breath against her cheek.

She had to force herself to maintain eye contact. "Yes, you would."

"If I buy a dozen, when I get down to four pairs I'll send out to the hotel laundry."

His voice vibrated down her spine as he moved another half step closer. It wasn't the direction she'd intended the conversation to take, but she didn't want it to end. "Compare the cost," she said after a deep, hard swallow, "of a dozen pairs of socks plus laundry fees against one pair you have to wash out." She felt like a sock in the wash herself, agitating in the dark blue of his eyes.

"I change when I go out at night. That means I'd have to wash two pairs every night."

"Well, yes."

"What if they don't get dry by morning?"

Now his face loomed directly over hers. A compelling face, a face she was afraid she would begin to see in her dreams, a face she'd like to simply reach up and kiss. Even as she felt her lips swell in anticipation, she heard herself say, "They will if you wring them out properly and pat most of the moisture out of them by wrapping them in a towel, but if you're that worried about it, maybe you need three pairs."

He stared at her for a long, long moment, his eyes melting her, his mouth an easily bridgeable inch from hers—then turned away. "Ring 'em up," he said to the salesman.

The kiss-op had ended and might never come back again. Mallory's spine felt like a single strand of angel-hair pasta. Carter's salesman gave Mallory a triumphant sneer. Out of the corner of her eye she saw her own salesman placing a burnt-orange sweater with blue diagonal stripes into a gift box. The sight of it stunned her. How had she managed to pick up that sweater? It looked like a University of Illinois pep squad uniform. Macon had been an undergraduate there, but he'd practically lived in the computer lab. He probably didn't know what a pep squad was. Had he even been aware there was a football team? He'd think she'd lost her mind.

Which was too true. Not only that, she'd blown it again with Carter. She didn't have a clue how to make him see her as a woman.

While she signed the sales slip for Macon's Amazing Christmas Surprise, Carter strolled off with his Big Brown Bag of socks. She wondered why his mother hadn't taught him a few basic things about packing for trips. Maybe he had a mother who knew other things, like which aria belonged to which opera. Still, sometime before Christmas she'd definitely slip him her copy of her mother's book.

Somehow she couldn't imagine Carter reading her mother's book. She couldn't imagine Carter going out with a woman who read her mother's books. This...this Athena person probably read—labels.

She could feel her mood darkening as rapidly as the afternoon sky. When she caught up with Carter at a display of hideously expensive shirts, his liveliness depressed her.

"My God, can you believe what people pay for stuff?" His gaze returned briefly to a last look at a navy-and-white-striped shirt with white collar and cuffs. "I did, too, once. I was twenty-five before I found out you could order a shirt from Lands' End for forty bucks that looks exactly like this one." He glanced at her. "All through here?"

"Yes," Mallory said, wondering if he knew the stripes in the shirt matched his eyes. He'd look great in it.

"What about a little Christmas cheer before we leave?"

"A drink?" *At this hour?*

"No, I meant go up to the Christmas floor. I like Christmas. You like Christmas?"

"Yes, of course." She felt embarrassed. Just because Carter forgot socks didn't mean he'd drink before five o'clock Central Standard Time.

She would have taken the elevator. He whisked her onto the escalator. "This will take longer," she couldn't help saying.

"We'll see more."

He was clearly not trainable. Just gorgeous, warm, utterly desirable...

"You'd look good in that dress."

She nearly decapitated herself leaning out over the escalator railing to see it. It was champagne-colored, clingy—and out of sight. "Umm," she said, and they continued upward, past sports clothes and more sports clothes, towels and sheets, china and silver, at last reaching a floor that smelled of bayberry and spice and glittered with heavily decorated trees.

They strolled through this fantasy land, Carter apparently enjoying himself, while Mallory tried not to think of the time they were wasting. Carter bought an ornament. Mallory rolled her eyes heavenward when she saw the price. While she was looking up, she noticed the balls of mistletoe hanging in each doorway. That's what she'd like to buy. She'd hang it in the doorway to her bedroom. Next time he yelled, "Mallory!" because he'd forgotten something, she'd open the door, stand directly under it and—

"Santa Claus is in the next room. Come on."

She had a crick in her neck. Rubbing it out, she followed him dumbly to the store Santa Claus who spied them and said, "Ho-ho-ho," in a thin, lonely sounding voice. The photographer sat in the store-fixture sleigh, hunched over an *F-Stop* magazine. It was a large room filled with shoppers, adults who seemed not to notice Santa as they grabbed up wrapping papers and ribbons, ornaments by the dozen.

"He's not getting much business," Carter whispered.

"I guess the kids are still in school. Or day care." Mallory glanced at her watch. "They have to wait until their parents come home from work to visit Santa." She was still obsessing on mistletoe.

Carter nodded, but said, "I feel sorry for him." He hesitated, then said, "Sit on his lap. Tell him what you want for Christmas." His hand nudged her elbow along.

"No, no," Mallory protested. "Don't be silly. Of course I'm not going to—"

"I dare you." A gleam in his dark blue eyes issued a challenge, but something else lay behind it—the certainty she'd refuse.

Could she rise to the challenge? Humiliate herself by doing something completely out of character?

It would certainly get Carter's attention, wouldn't it, and wasn't that what she wanted?

Without another thought, she made a beeline for Santa and perched herself on his lap. Behind her, she heard the most satisfying sound in the world, a sharp gasp of surprise from Carter. Once she was on Santa's red velour knees and could spin around to see a small and amused audience gathering, she saw he looked uneasy.

Good. Let him feel uneasy for once in his disgustingly self-confident life.

"Ho, ho, ho," Santa Claus said. "Well, have you been a good little girl this year?"

"Entirely too good," Mallory said, "which may be my problem..." She stopped short, realizing this wasn't a therapy session.

"Ho, ho, ho," Santa said, shifting a little in his tapestry wing chair. "So what does this *very* good little girl want for Christmas?"

Mallory let her gaze wander back to Carter. The group gathered around him was larger now, and he seemed edgy. Edgy but sexier than ever with his arms crossed over his broad chest and a slight frown drawing his dark eyebrows down in the middle and up at the ends.

She suddenly knew what she wanted. She knew with a confidence every bit as disgusting as Carter's. By Christmas, she would make him see her as a woman, a feminine, desirable, irresistible woman, or die trying.

"I want him," she whispered in Santa's ear. "I want Carter for Christmas."

4

As she sat on Santa's lap, a hot flush of humiliation climbing her face, the last thing Mallory expected to hear Santa say was "Him? Ooh. I can't blame you."

It was not a Santa-like thing to say. Mallory took a close look into his appropriately blue eyes.

"Ho, ho, ho," he boomed suddenly, then threw her off balance again by whispering, "You mentioned a problem. So what's the problem? You're a dish, he's a hunk, you're both single, I presume. And straight." He sighed.

It was not a Santa-like sigh. "I'm not a dish," Mallory said, giving him another close look.

"Please don't report me," Santa said. "I shouldn't have said 'dish.' I know better. Santa Claus is politically correct."

"Oh, think nothing of it," Mallory assured him, realizing he was a New York Santa, not a Midwestern Santa, and she should be sophisticated enough to adjust to slight differences in mannerisms. "I meant I'm not beautiful or sexy or any of the things I need to be to attract him." She crooked her neck in Carter's direction.

"Who says?" Santa's eyes got very big behind his silver-rimmed spectacles.

"I says. I mean, I know I'm not." The more whispering she and Santa did, the deeper Carter's frown became. "My boss says I'm not. He—" this time she sent her thumb in Carter's direction "—treats me like I'm not. So I'm not. I'm frumpy and dull and when he looks at me, he sees a—a law book."

"Sounds like Santa needs to give him glasses for Christmas," Santa muttered.

"No, Santa needs to give me—" she stopped and thought for a second "—a whole new image," she finally got out. "I want to turn into a sex goddess."

"By Christmas."

"That's my target date."

"This is so serendipitous," Santa breathed. "If it were in a book, nobody would believe it."

"Believe what?" He wasn't merely a New York Santa. He was truly a very odd Santa.

"That you need help and I know exactly where to send you to get it." He darted a glance at the growing crowd, and apparently motivated by Carter's thunderous expression, almost knocked Mallory off his lap with his next hearty "Ho-ho-ho." Then he dug into his pocket and pulled out a peppermint and a card. "Call this number," he whispered, then shouted enthusiastically, "Merry Christmas."

Deafened by the sound, Mallory tucked the card into the breast pocket of her jacket and slid off his padded lap. If a department store Santa Claus had just referred her to a psychiatrist, that would be absolutely the last straw.

ON THE WAY BACK to the hotel, Carter was unusually silent. Not that Mallory could have heard him if he'd been chatting companionably away. They'd emerged from Bloomingdale's to find the streets jammed with honking cars and the sidewalks packed with shoppers. Their Brown Bags jostled with Saks Fifth Avenue red ones, Bergdorf Goodman's handsome navy totes, Lord & Taylor white ones printed in red script, Gucci, FAO Schwartz and Sony bags.

Through narrowed eyes she caught the glances women sent toward Carter as he effortlessly cut a path through the crowd, snowflakes dusting his navy overcoat and dark hair, while Mallory struggled to keep up with him. From time to time she peeked into her own Medium Brown Bag at the gift box that held Macon's sweater. Burnt orange. Blue stripes. A shudder passed through her. While she'd inherited her mother's Nordic blondness, Macon took after their father, a symphony in browns, chestnut hair, interesting amber eyes, olive skin. The pale beige V-necked sweater would have been perfect for him. What was he going to do with a—

Save receipts at least three months. File them under Appliances, Gifts, Services and Personal. You never know when you may have to return an inappropriate gift or faulty appliance, or demand that a job done poorly be done over.

Ellen Trent again. One of her major rules for a well-run life. Until that thought popped into Mallory's mind, her first priority had been to look at the business card Santa had slipped her. Now the worry that she might have forgotten her receipt took precedence.

Surreptitiously she began to grope around in the bag. When Carter cast a glance in her direction, she suspended her search, then resumed it when he wasn't looking. She didn't want him to know she was obsessing over a receipt, didn't want him to know she'd been rattled enough to buy a sweater she was already thinking of returning.

At last she thrust her hand all the way down to the bottom of the bag where her gloved fingertips snagged a loose corner of paper and tugged on it.

The receipt. She glanced at it, gasped and came to a dead halt at the corner of Fifty-ninth Street. The crowd rear-ended her, righted itself, then divided like the Red Sea, casting nasty looks at her as they swarmed around her. Carter, who'd been turning the corner, cut himself out of the pack and fought his way back in her direction.

"What happened? Whoa. Where are you going?" he said as she whirled.

"Back to Bloomingdale's," she said.

He contemplated her for a moment. "You have a thing for Santa Claus, huh?"

The snowflakes that whirled through the air swarmed on her eyelashes, and she blinked hard to clear them. When she saw his gaze riveted on them, she batted them again, more deliberately this time. "Maybe," she said.

His jaw tightened. "I'll see you back at the hotel."

"You may have gone out with Athena by the time I get back, so—"

"Who? Oh. Athena."

"So we should decide now on a time to meet in the morning."

"We're due at Phoebe Angell's office at nine. What about going down to breakfast at seven-thirty." It wasn't a question.

"I'll be ready. You'll be home by then?" she said, and it *was* a question.

He gazed at her for a moment before he said, "Maybe," and with a slight wave, joined the lemmings swimming east toward the St. Regis on Fifth Avenue.

Jostled by the annoyed shoppers who stepped around her, she watched him go, standing tall in the crowd, the wind rustling his crisp, dark hair, his step sure and purposeful. No wonder she'd just paid $425—plus tax, when she could have saved the tax by having it shipped—for the ugliest sweater in the universe. Proximity to Carter made it difficult to remember anything, even how to spend money wisely.

Everyone should have a budget and stick to it. Financial worries reduce one's efficiency and—

"Shut up, Mother," Mallory muttered, and charged through the crowd toward Bloomie's.

"MY FAITH IN MANKIND is restored," said the clerk when she returned the sweater. She watched him pluck it up with two fingers and put it aside, a look of distaste on his face. "Good decision." Stepping out of the men's department, her pace slowed. She really didn't want to go back to the suite. Listening through a closed door to Carter getting ready for his date with Athena would be depressing. Pretending to get ready for an imaginary date of her own would be even more depressing.

Slowly she pulled the card Santa had given her out of her pocket. "M. Ewing," it said. "ImageMakers." Below that, in both quotes and italics, it said, *"A new you in no time flat."*

Mallory drew her brows together. The words were engraved on heavy, expensive card stock. The address was one on the Upper East Side, a high-rent district. "A new you in no time flat" was a jarring addition to the otherwise elegant presentation of the card. "Be the person you want to be," maybe, or "Realize your personal potential." Something like that would have sounded more appropriate.

Still, this person claimed to be an imagemaker and came personally recommended by Santa Claus himself. Mallory knew what an imagemaker did. Was that what she needed? Somebody to help her show the world outside she was a woman—a passionate woman?

Forget the world outside. Her sights were fixed on one person in the world. She had her target date and her target victim. Damn straight an overnight imagemaker was what she needed. If M. Ewing turned out to be a charlatan, she'd be out—what? A few hundred dollars? Which she'd just saved by returning the sweater. Without another minute's consideration, she darted into a small nook devoted to a display of Chanel handbags in their leathery, unaffordable splendor. Ignoring the scornful gaze of the woman behind the counter—an armed guard, probably, given the cost of these handbags—she dialed the number listed on the card.

"ImageMakers," purred a smooth male voice. "Richard Gifford speaking. May I help you?"

The voice went with the card. The address went with the card. The only thing that didn't go with the card was that "A new you in no time flat." "I'd like an appointment." Mallory's tone matched this Richard person's in cool professionalism. "That is, if Mr. or Ms Ewing sees clients in the evenings, because I'm only available then."

"Ms. Ewing sees clients at their convenience." A pause ensued. Richard was obviously consulting a schedule. "Her next evening appointment is on February 9. Shall I—"

Why had she assumed she could mosey on over to become a new her in no time flat, like, right now? "I'm sorry," she said, "but I'm visiting here and—"

"Who referred you to us?" The man's interest seemed to have picked up.

It burst out of her mouth. "Santa Claus."

"Right. Ms. Ewing has had a sudden cancellation. She can see you this evening. As in now. When shall we expect you?"

Mallory felt dazed, and possibly conned. But she felt committed to an image change and she wasn't going to let herself cop out.

"How fortunate," she said. "I'll be there—" She glanced at her watch. The afternoon had flown. "I'll be there at seven."

It wasn't far. Ten minutes ought to do it.

She was committed. Wondering if she should just commit herself to some kindly healing institution instead, she started out of the store, then screeched to a halt, spun and sped back to the men's department. A few minutes later she had paid $165 for a dark-blue-and-white-striped shirt in a very large size.

She'd also used seven of her ten minutes. *Punctuality is key to your success in life. Arrive when you say you'll arrive, and give yourself some leeway for the odd traffic jam, something you can't control—*

"Mother," Mallory muttered to herself as she tossed her credit card into any old corner of her purse it chose to land in, "I already told you. Bug off. I'm in over your head."

While she knew that Sixty-seventh Street just off Fifth Avenue would be an area of nice houses, she wasn't prepared for a Beaux Arts mansion. Typical of Manhattan residences, it was small as mansions went.

Mallory clutched her black cashmere coat more tightly around herself and went up to the huge double doors.

There was no box of buttons and buzzers, no list of doctors or dentists or psychiatrists who had made this once-proud single-family residence their professional home. There seemed no alternative but to knock, which one did by grasping a long, pendulous brass thing and banging it against the two brass spheres beneath it. Mallory did a double take, and was having second thoughts about the wisdom of this project when the door opened and a glorious figure of a man said, "Like the knocker? I picked it out myself." Without waiting for an answer, he added, "Come in. Ms. Ewing will see you at once."

"But I—"

"I'll take your coat."

"Thank you. I—"

"Follow me, please."

Giving up, she followed him through a massive foyer, across a marble floor, under a sparkling chandelier and past a sweeping staircase and a few pieces of furniture that looked as if they should be sporting Don't Touch signs. Richard swept open both halves of a tall, curtained French door, said, "Ms. Trent to see you," and steered Mallory ahead of him and into the room.

"Hey, hon," said a voice. "Come on in and set yourself down."

One look at the woman behind the desk and Mallory knew she was in the wrong place. She turned to flee, but Richard blocked her path. She turned back. "You know," she said in a quavering voice, "maybe this isn't the right thing for me to do just now at such an extremely busy point in my life."

"*Au contraire,*" Ms. Ewing said, drawling the words out to their legal limit. "Looks to me like y'all got here in the nick of time."

Dragging her feet, Mallory headed for the chair opposite the desk. It was an ordinary chair, and she felt slightly better sitting down. The desk, on the other hand, was an alarming concoction of branches and horns, or antlers maybe, topped by a slab of stone that looked as if it should have crushed the desk to mulch and bone meal upon installation. But the desk, at least, had the good grace not to speak. If it had spoken, it would probably have mooed. Even that would have been better than listening to Ms. Ewing's exaggerated country-music star accent.

She was a tiny woman with an enormous head of teased, gelled and sprayed blond hair. Half woman, half hair. Her face was thin and sharp-featured. Her eyes, huge and blue, surprised Mallory with their gleam of intelligence. And her mouth, a narrow hot-pink slash across her tanned, weather-beaten face, quirked up at the corners. She could be fifty, she could be ninety. It was that hard to tell.

This is a house of prostitution and I've just met my first madam.

Or I'm being interviewed for a rodeo.

As if her legs had springs, Mallory tensed herself for action. But first, she had to distract the woman from her true intention, which was to flee. "What an interesting desk, Ms. Ewing," she said, leaning forward, getting her Soft 'N' Comfy pumps in position to push off the Oriental rug.

"Maybelle, hon, jes' call me Maybelle, and for goodness' sake, relax. Y'all look like you're about to run."

Caught like a shoplifter with a mascara up her

sleeve, Mallory tried to look less obvious. Still staring at Maybelle, she had to admit that the woman's simple black jacket looked expensive. All she could see of the blouse beneath it was the neckline of something in a snakeskin print. Nothing alarming about that.

"And don't worry about them horns. Some of 'em fell off the critters natural-like and the other ones got what they deserved. Want some coffee?"

Mallory hesitated. At least Maybelle hadn't offered her a controlled substance. "Do you have decaffeinated?"

Maybelle sighed. "Another one of *them*. Honest to gosh, you young folks," she said, then screamed, "*Dickie!*" Mallory levitated straight up out of her chair, but Maybelle went on in her normal nasal twang. "Y'all stay up all night, but you're scared to death of caffeine."

Richard reappeared. "You rang?" he said eloquently.

"Got another one of them decaf drinkers. Perk us up a pot, will ya, sugar?"

"It's already brewing," Richard, or Dickie, replied. He gave Mallory a look that said, "Isn't she something?" over the top of Maybelle's head. "Maybelle, I told you she wouldn't want your fully leaded stuff."

Maybelle looked discontentedly after him as he vanished, his big frame silent as a cat's. "Nobody wants real coffee anymore," she said. "The kind that's perked on the stove and reheated 'til it's like axle grease. Now that's coffee you can sink your teeth into."

Mallory began to worry again. Her good manners told her she had to stay long enough for the cup of coffee she'd just custom-ordered, but no longer than that, and there were a couple of things she had to get straight before she revealed anything about herself to this supposed imagemaker, who looked and sounded as if she could use one of her own. "What do you charge for your services?"

"We don' need to tawk about that jes' yet," Maybelle said with a wave of a diamond-studded hand.

Mallory heard a loud throat-clearing sound, then Richard reappeared, positioning himself behind Maybelle like a bodyguard. "Ms. Ewing charges one hundred dollars an hour and prefers to see new clients daily for the first week, tapering off in subsequent weeks," he intoned, sounding like a recording. "She'll see you each evening at seven and at four on weekends until further notice. A typical client can expect a fee of about two thousand dollars. Cream and sugar?" he added, circling the desk with the silver tray he'd been holding while he did his piece.

"Black, thanks."

Maybelle smiled. "Way-ell, there's some hope for ya."

Mallory frowned back. There was one more thing she had to know. "What sort of training did you have for this business?" she said, trying hard to say it nicely, as if she were merely interested in Maybelle's background.

"Training?" Maybelle cackled. "No need to worry yourself about that, hon. I got me plenty of trainin' in all kinds of things. Look at them diplomas." She cocked a thumb over her shoulder as Richard drifted out of the room.

Mallory gripped the handle of an exquisite bone china teacup as if it were the only piece of debris at hand after a shipwreck, and she directed her gaze to the wall behind Maybelle. It was papered with diplomas in gilded frames.

She narrowed her eyes. Diplomas could easily be faked. She had a strong feeling that the woman behind the desk wouldn't hesitate to buy diplomas by the square foot.

"And besides," Maybelle was saying, "look at me." She stood up.

That was the problem. Mallory *was* looking at her. The woman topped out at five feet, and below the elegant black jacket Mallory saw pressed light blue jeans and a pair of heeled boots that upped the definition of cowboy boots by a quantum leap. They were black, tooled in yellow and purple pansies.

Mallory blinked, hesitated, left her saucer on the edge of the desk and stood, still holding the cup by its delicate handle. She carefully walked around the desk, narrowly avoiding being gored by a protruding horn, to join Maybelle at the wall.

Many of the diplomas were from correspondence schools and announced Maybelle's successful completion of courses in an amazing variety of fields, from mathematics to pottery-making. "Don't pay them no mind," Maybelle said, dismissing them with a wave. The enormous diamonds in her rings sent rainbows across the high ceiling of the room. "I took them courses to inner-tain and edgy-cate myself after Hadley died. My husband," she explained.

"I'm sorry," Mallory said.

"I was, too," Maybelle said, "and real bored without him around to fight with." She moved on down the wall and so did Mallory.

Here there were diplomas written in Chinese characters and a diploma from the Parsons School of Design. "You were an interior designer?" Mallory said, casting a glance back at the desk.

"Oh, my, yeah," Maybelle said. "That was the most fun I ever had."

"And lucrative," Mallory murmured, trying to imagine a house this woman had had a hand in decorating, trying to imagine her on the loose in China. She couldn't even speak English.

"Way-ell, no." Maybelle looked reflective. "The money never interested me very much. But I do get bored real easy, so next I got me a Ph.D. in Clinical Psychology—"

The coffee sloshed onto Mallory's only pair of black trousers.

"—then an MBA, so's I'd know what y'all young folks was up against in the business world. What line of work did you say you was in?"

The psychology degree was from Johns Hopkins and the MBA from New York University. "I'm a lawyer," Mallory said, feeling humbled.

"I may get me one of them degrees next," Maybelle declared. "Dickie's significant other? He's involved in this lawsuit with a whole bunch of other people, and I want to tell you, that lawyer's gonna make out good."

Mallory tensed up. "Ah, what kind of lawsuit?"

Maybelle stepped toward her desk and Mallory followed. "The craziest thing happened," Maybelle said as she settled herself down. "He's got the show biz bug, and he was going to audition for this part where they wanted a redhead—"

It couldn't be. It just couldn't.

"Now that we've gotten to know each other, mind if I take off this jacket?" Maybelle interrupted herself, taking it off without waiting for Mallory to answer.

"Of course—" she looked down at the T-shirt beneath the jacket "—not." The T-shirt wasn't your customary snakeskin print. It depicted a python wrapped around Maybelle's skinny body, its head curling down over one shoulder.

"—and the stuff dyed his hair green."

"No!" Mallory said, breaking eye contact with the python as she realized she had something worse than snakes to worry about.

"Oh, yes," Maybelle said, misunderstanding Mallory's explosive response. "And he's real thorough about his character development, y'know? So he didn't just dye the hair on his head, nosirree. He dyed everything, if y'all get my drift."

Mallory, perched at the very edge of her chair, said, "You mean—"

"I mean for a while there even his little tallywhacker was green," Maybelle said. "And I want to tell y'all he was mighty put out." She paused for a moment. "They have an apartment here in the house. The tawk gets kindly personal sometimes."

"Maybelle, there's something I have to tell you," Mallory began. How could Maybelle help her if she had a conflict of interests?

Maybelle leaned forward. "Well, of course you do, and here I am chattering on about stuff. Y'all came here for help. Help gettin' your man, a little bird told me. Sounds to me like a real intrestin' project."

Silently Mallory weighed her choices. This woman might be crazy as a cat on uppers, but she did have all those degrees and all those diamonds, and she did have intelligent eyes. Why did she have to know that Mallory was on the opposite side of her housemate's lawsuit? Only because Mallory felt morally obligated to tell her. But why? If Maybelle herself were involved in the case, that would be different, but—

While her mind went around in circles, Maybelle rattled on. "I don't know what you're so worried about. You're purty. You seem smart. Whatcha want to change?"

Locations? Go back to the hotel and remember this experience as nothing more than a very interesting evening? The conclusion she came to, after weighing all the evidence, was that in the course of one momentous day she'd sat on Santa's lap, she'd made herself come here, she'd faced up to a doorknocker that looked like Andre the Giant naked and she hadn't run away. She might never have this much courage again. *It's now or never.* "Me," Mallory whispered. "I want to change me, from the inside out."

5

"The wedding was a hoot," Athena said. "I had to compete with all that Eurotrash the princess runs around with and I knew there wasn't a designer on the face of this earth who would impress them, so I went down to the West Forties and bought just tons and tons of silk chiffon in a bunch of colors, and then I—"

Maybe she's had lipo and they accidentally suctioned out her brain along with the fat. Carter forced a smile toward the gorgeous creature sitting opposite him at Le Bernardin. Athena was six feet tall and even skinnier than she'd been the last time he saw her, when she'd weighed maybe ninety-six pounds. The dinner she wasn't eating would cost him $250, easy.

"—Fashion Institute, and he just swirled it all around me like a toga." Athena paused briefly. "Sort of like a toga, because togas are usually white, aren't they? But this wasn't—this was all those colors I picked out, so—"

Thank you for clarifying. He tried to imagine having a conversation like this with Mallory, but he couldn't. *Wonder who Mallory's going out with. Somebody she's known a long time? A family friend? A relative?*

It was true that he and Mallory had had a conversation about socks. What had that scene in the sock department been all about? She'd come prissing over to interfere in his sock purchase—like she knew better than he did how many socks he needed—and standing there, feeling pretty annoyed by her know-it-all attitude, he'd had the strangest urge to kiss her. The closer he'd gotten to her, the stronger the urge had become. He'd had to get a firm grip on himself to keep from giving her a sizzling one right there in the store.

Then he'd gotten all upset again when she and Santa Claus had done all that whispering to each other. What, he wanted to know, were they whispering about? *Did Santa Claus ask her for a date?* Carter had been slouching, but this thought bolted him upright in his chair. The way the guy had come on to her—it didn't seem ethical. Santa Claus was supposed to be faithful to Mrs. Claus. Carter drew his eyebrows together.

"When that anorexic bimbo Simonetta saw me, she screamed. Then she ran up to me and said, 'Who did that divine dress?' but she said it in Italian, and I thought she was trying to attack me for outbidding her on that apartment she wanted, so I got really mad and was about to start pulling her hair, but Fernando rushed up in the nick of time and told me what she'd said in English—"

"Dessert?" Carter said, hoping he didn't sound as desperate as he felt.

"Soon as I finish telling you," Athena said. "So I told her I'd found a brand-new designer and wasn't telling anybody about him until I was sure I had his absolute and total loyalty." She pursed her glossy, puffy lips into a stern line.

"You stole her apartment," Carter said. "Don't you think you owe her a dress designer?" *Good God, I'm getting into the conversation. Another ten minutes and I'll be asking her if she thinks I'm more a Brioni type or a—who is that other guy, the one with the sloppy doublebreasted suits? Ambrose. Armand. That's it, I think, Ar—*

Athena stamped her four-inch spike of a heel on the floor beneath the table. It was dramatic enough to make him jump. "There was no designer," she said in a newly gritty voice. "He was just a student at the Fashion Institute of Technology. That was the whole point, that I did something really creative and knocked the lace Wolford stockings off Simonetta, and you weren't even listening."

"I was," he protested. "He wrapped you up like a toga. I mean, the stuff you bought, he wrapped it around you like a toga of many colors." He was pretty embarrassed about his manners. When you dated around, as he did, you were bound to have one of these bored-to-catatonia nights once in a while, but you learned to act decent for the duration of the catastrophe and just not call the woman again.

He must have enjoyed his last date with Athena or he wouldn't have called her again. Funny, he couldn't remember his last date with Athena.

"I was gorgeous." Athena's voice went up another notch. "I *am* gorgeous. And you aren't paying the slightest bit of attention to me." She stood up. "I wouldn't eat your dessert if it were the last dessert anyone ever offered me. I'm going to meet Fernando at the Fressen bar. He pays attention to me." She cast disapproving eyes down as much of him as she could see. "He," she added as a final blow, "wears Armani."

That's the guy's name, Armani. Regretting nothing but the fact that he had been rude to Athena and had forgotten a household word like *Armani,* Carter summoned the waiter.

Dinner, now that he thought back on it, had mainly

consisted of a lot of plates. On the way back to the St. Regis, he bought and devoured a Double Meat, Double Cheese Bigger Burger with plenty of mustard from the packets he'd stashed in his pockets.

It was significant that he couldn't remember the last date he'd had with Athena. One thing for sure, there wouldn't be another one. Brie, now Brie was a hard-working, sensible girl, a bond salesperson on Wall Street. They'd eat steak and she'd order hers rare. Tomorrow night would go better.

He wondered how Mallory's night was going. If Santa Claus had asked her out, Carter swore he'd report it to the store manager.

AFTER HER LECTURE from Maybelle, Mallory was still feeling stubborn about the woman's insistence that she wear Carol's red jacket tomorrow. It was too sexy for the work scene, Mallory had argued. She'd buy something a little brighter in a day or two.

However, since she'd told Carter she was going out for the evening, she'd better look as if she'd just gotten home if he came in unexpectedly. So she switched her black pants for the black skirt and the black shell for the white one and put her jacket back on. She was in the sitting room working and paying a little attention to a movie on television when she heard a keycard slice into the lock and saw the door open. Startled, she looked up. "Carter. You're home early." Just seeing him made her heart do a flip-flop.

"You got home first." He glared at her. "Was it a great date?"

"Just fabulous," she said with a smile she hoped would mislead him. "But I got to thinking about the case."

"Me, too." He sounded grumpy. "I'm going to take my stuff into my room and work awhile."

She jumped up. "You can work here. I'll go to *my* room. I thought you'd be—"

"Well, I wasn't. I'm home, okay? But stay where you are."

"No, no, I'll..." He was looking at her so impatiently she trailed off, deciding to drop it. His door slammed, and the suite fell into silence.

Mallory lowered the volume on the movie one more increment and went back to reading the full account of Sensuous's early attempts to settle the Green case with its green complainants. It still seemed to her that her company's offer had been extremely generous. Ms. Angell had seen her chance, though, and had convinced the clients she'd rounded up that being green could be worth millions.

As Maybelle had implied, Ms. Angell was the one who would be worth millions when the dust settled. Lawyers.

She was a lawyer, too. What was she doing, criticizing the habits of members of her own profession? But she would not personally do what Ms. Angell was doing, and she was fairly sure Carter wouldn't, either. Of course, how did she know what Carter would or would not do?

He hadn't enjoyed his date with Athena enough to spend the night with her, and Mallory was simply thrilled. *And* he'd been curious about her "date." That was even more thrilling.

She looked down at herself. Maybe Maybelle was right. It would be pretty hard to believe she'd had a hot, intense encounter with anybody in these clothes. She was more appropriately dressed to give a speech to a kindergarten class. But the red jacket was just too, too—

"Mallory!" A shout came from Carter's room. "Do you have a—" his door burst open "—copy of *Lindon v. Hanson*, you know, that other hair-dye case—"

"Right here." Mallory fumbled for the printout in her briefcase. In his sock feet, with his shirt half open, Carter looked rumpled, sleepy and devastatingly desirable. She pulled out the document and with it, a half dozen sheets of paper that fluttered to the floor.

He swept them up with one large hand. "I told Brenda to copy it to my laptop, but I guess she didn't. Or she filed it somewhere only she could find it." He'd lowered his voice to a grumble. "I don't know why nobody does anything right anymore. They just aim it and see if it flies. Hey, what's this?"

Mallory could see what he was holding and felt deeply embarrassed, her privacy violated. "Um, that's my, ah, packing list, or wardrobe schedule, I guess you'd call it. Here's your—"

"So that's how you do it, pack in a briefcase. 'Tuesday—black pants, jacket, black shell. Wednesday—black skirt, jacket, white shell, scarf. Thursday, Friday, Monday'—what do you do over the weekend? Go naked?" He waggled his eyebrows suggestively.

She gritted her teeth to hide the shiver that ran through her. "Not in the wintertime. I wear the black pants with a sweater. Give me that."

He waved her off. "'Monday—black jacket, black skirt, cream shell.' Hey, the black jacket's sure getting a workout."

"You only need one black jacket." She viewed him coldly.

"What if something happens to it?"

"Nothing happens to a black wool jacket you can't fix with a little cool water."

"Nothing?"

"If it does, you send it out for a rush cleaning."

He narrowed his eyes. "What if it's too much of a rush? What if, for example, something happened right now? You honestly think the hotel is going to get a jacket cleaned and back to you by morning?"

"Well, no, but what could happen?" He was fishing in his pants pocket and, for some reason, it made her nervous.

"Oh, maybe something like this." In one swift gesture he tore a corner off a small plastic packet and aimed the opening in her direction.

Blobs of yellow flew through the air and plopped onto her clothes. She leaped up. "Carter! This is...this is...*mustard!*"

He gave her a wicked smile. "Right. Now what are you going to do?"

"I am going to my room," she said frostily, and did.

There she viewed the ruin of the jacket she'd planned to wear every single day. There were a few spots on her skirt she could probably handle, or she could wear her black pants again, which smelled only faintly of the coffee she'd spilled on them in Maybelle's office, but even if she got the mustard off the coat, she'd smell like a delicatessen all day tomorrow.

She buried her head in her hands. She'd have to wear the red jacket, after all.

CARTER OPENED HIS bedroom door warily to find Mallory emerging from her room looking as if she were expecting an ambush. He met her in the center of the room, where they eyed each other like opposing lines in a football game.

Mallory's team was the one in red. He cleared his throat. "You did have something else to wear."

"Fortunately." She brandished the ruined black jacket.

He hadn't gotten a rip-roaring, let's-laugh-it-off, no-harm-done conversation going, that was for sure, but, wow, was she ever a bombshell in red. A surprisingly curvy, sexy red number that fired up the old imagination, and that wasn't all it fired up.

Feeling the need for something to hold over himself, he said, "Give me that." He took the jacket, stuffed it in the plastic bag the hotel provided and stuck it outside the door of the suite. "The laundry will pick it up and have it back tonight. It'll be on my bill," he added, and by the time he'd done all that practical stuff, he felt more in control. And increasingly foolish as she eyed him silently.

"What were you thinking?" she said at last.

"I don't know. The devil made me do it?"

"Why did you have mustard in your pocket? Did you take Athena out for hamburgers?"

"No, Athena and I had some very pricey raw fish. Then I took myself out for a hamburger."

"Oh." She shouldered a gleaming black leather handbag, grabbed the handle of her rolling briefcase and started toward the door. She glanced back at him briefly. "Thank you for having coffee sent up early."

"I thought it might help us get going." He stubbed a toe into the carpeting, and that brilliant bit of conversation didn't net him any response at all.

His role was to follow her to the elevators, which he did, feeling like an embarrassed kid shuffling along in her wake. What had made him do something so childish as to squirt mustard on her? He hadn't been in a food fight since his sophomore year in high school. When a very pretty junior girl told him what a "sophomoric" thing it was to do, that had ended his food-fighting forever. So this bizarre behavior of his must have something to do with the mood he'd come home in after enduring two hours of Athena's empty blathering to find Mallory all neat and dressed and *working*. Could she never fail to one-up him? That mood, plus the effect she was having on him, were making him feel like a kid again—and not in a nice way.

But while he stared at her back, thinking these thoughts, he made an important discovery. She had the cutest, roundest little butt any man could hope to find on a woman. He hadn't realized he was a butt man, but now it seemed he was. Suddenly she turned, and he whipped his gaze upward, but not before she caught him staring at her rear end.

She flushed and gave him a grim look. The tips of his ears felt hot and he tried to return her look with a nonchalant one.

Great start on getting her to respect you. All he'd accomplished so far was to make Mallory look a little less respectable in that sexy red jacket. The jacket that showed her butt. *Quit it, Compton.* They'd landed in the lobby, and he could smell eggs and bacon, hear clanking silverware. He intended to have a huge breakfast

She'd be sitting down. That would help. If he could keep his eyes off the neckline. It plunged down between her breasts, which the jacket pushed out and clung to. Thank God she was wearing one of those things she called "shells" underneath it.

Heat was traveling through him in waves, and this

was only breakfast. He had to keep his hands off her. If he didn't, her respect for him would decrease to an all-time low. He was tough. He was strong. He could do it. No problem.

"MS. ANGELL," CARTER said, and held out his hand. "Carter Compton."

"Mallory Trent," Mallory said, and held out her hand. "Glad to meet you in person at last after all our phone con..." She trailed off. The problem was that Phoebe Angell was still holding Carter's hand and appeared to be melting right there in front of both of them.

She was as tall as Mallory and there the resemblance ended. Phoebe Angell had raven's-wing hair in a short cut that stuck up in various directions, snapping black eyes, skin like almond custard, gunmetal-gray lipstick and fingernails, and a black leather skirt short enough to get a lawyer disbarred in Illinois. She wore it with a surprisingly proper, perfectly pressed white shirt. Her shoes were red, with trendy pointed toes and four-inch heels. In a word, she was dramatic.

Mallory supposed she could dress this way because she'd gone into practice with her father. The law offices of Angell and Angell had a prestigious midtown location on a high floor. With just the two of them plus a support staff of aides and paralegals, the suite wasn't large, but it was luxurious. Mallory wondered what was driving Phoebe Angell so hard, why she seemed to feel that winning this case would be the turning point in her professional life.

The three of them stood just inside Phoebe's office where Phoebe had greeted them. An enormous portrait of Alphonse Angell himself dominated the wall opposite her desk. A formidable-looking man, he hadn't even managed a smile for his portrait. Mallory wondered how Phoebe got any work done under the vigilant scrutiny of his cold black eyes. She shivered. It was possible Alphonse Angell could win in a face-off against her own father. Maybe even against her mother, and that was saying something. She felt a flash of sympathy for Phoebe Angell, which she quashed, mainly because Phoebe was still clinging to Carter's hand.

Having assessed the opposition with her own hand still flapping around emptily in front of her, Mallory sent a sidelong glance toward the man who was supposed to be on her side. Maybe it was just wishful thinking, but he did seem to be trying to get his hand back, and his smile was still an impersonal one.

"Thank you, Phoebe," Mallory said sharply, giving up on the possibility of a handshake, "for offering us your conference room for the depositions."

"Hmm?" Phoebe said dreamily. "Oh, yes." She released Carter and regained her poise with admirable speed, herding them toward the conference room in question, which was several doors down from her office. "It seemed the sensible thing to do, to depose the plaintiffs here since they live close by. The green dye was all in Lot Number 12867 which was shipped to New Jersey."

We know that. Mallory kept her gaze level with the woman's eyes.

"And besides," Phoebe said, sealing her fate with Mallory, "I've never known a Midwesterner who wasn't looking for a junket to New York. And I have to say I can't blame you." She rolled her eyes, dismissing the Midwestern work ethic, standards and values,

Marshall Fields, the best pizza in the world and Frank Lloyd Wright architecture in that one gesture. Mallory didn't know where to start—"It's not a junket," "Keep your hands off Carter" or "I'll meet you out back by the Dumpster and we'll see about changing your attitude toward the Midwest."

Carter's elbow nudged her. She was sure it was accidental that he nudged her just below her breast. Nonetheless, it took the breath out of her, so she didn't say or do anything drastic, just surreptitiously hiked her skirt up a bit.

"Will your father be involved in the case?" she asked Phoebe, hoping to distract both her and Carter from the little alteration project she was attempting by sliding her hand up under the red jacket and turning over her waistband.

"Father's involved in a big case in Minneapolis," Phoebe said abruptly. "He won't be on the premises. I'll be discussing the case with him, of course. He's very interested in it." Her eyes darted toward her own office, where the portrait hung.

"We're going to depose Tammy Sue Teezer this morning, right?" Carter said, starting to layer the table with the contents of his briefcase.

"Right," said Phoebe. "She'll be here in a few minutes. The court reporter's already here and so is the cameraman. I've arranged for coffee and pastries this morning, sandwiches and cookies this afternoon. If you have time to get started with Kevin Knightson, he'll be on hand at one o'clock. Anything else?"

"That should take care of us," Carter said. "We'll get set up."

"Yell if you need anything before Tammy Sue arrives," Phoebe said, curling herself around the doorframe and finally disappearing.

"Junket," Mallory muttered.

"Black Widow spider's what she is," Carter whispered. "Her plaintiffs must have been putty in her hands."

"Slime," Mallory said. "It's green."

"Good joke," Carter said without a hint of amusement in his voice. "Now, I'm going to put the witness at the head of the table and I'm going to sit to the side. You sit on my left, the court reporter asked for her own little table, which is there." He pointed. "The cameraman gets the foot of the table with a direct view of the witness and the Black Widow can sit beside her client. How about that skirt? I can't imagine you going to work in a skirt like that."

Get ready for a surprise, mister. The thought careened wildly through Mallory's mind and crashed against her skull. Was she actually thinking of following Maybelle's advice, of tarting herself up to get Carter's attention?

He'd certainly been fascinated by her rear end this morning.

A soft ache slid down her body as she remembered the hot glitter in his eyes when she caught him staring. And what had she done? She'd glowered at him. Even if she fine-tuned her outside, she'd still have a lot of work to do on the inside.

"Earth to Mallory."

"Oh, sorry," she said. "The arrangement sounds fine. Tammy Sue Teezer," she added. "Can that possibly be her real name?"

"That question's on my list," Carter said.

"I'M ALL SET," SAID THE cameraman. From his position at the foot of the table, he would videotape the depositions. If the case went to trial, the jury could view the tape to see the witnesses in person.

"Ms. White?" Carter said to the court reporter, a middle-aged woman who sat poised over her shorthand machine.

"Ready to go," she said.

"Bring in the first witness," Carter said.

Phoebe appeared at the door with a woman who was probably not as young as she seemed at first glance. Her black leather skirt was shorter than Phoebe's and her biker jacket was half leather, half zippers. Her hair was short, curly and a peculiar shade of green at the ends. The peculiar shade could probably be explained by the fact that the hair that had grown out was bleached almost white. The peroxide hadn't taken out the green, just toned it down some.

"Hi," she said, struck a pose for the cameraman, then sat down and splayed out fingernails that were red in the middle and green around the edges.

She made quite an impression. "Good morning, Miss Teezer," Carter said, and choked. Damn it, he was going to laugh. He darted a desperate look at Mallory, who sent back a repressive frown. He managed to introduce himself and her, then said, "Try to relax. You're not on trial here. We're all just friends and business associates trying to come to an equitable solution to a difficult problem."

It would be hard to imagine anyone more relaxed than Tammy Sue. She sat back in her chair, rested one booted foot on the other knee and popped her chewing gum.

"State your full name, please, for the court reporter."

"Like I said, Tammy Sue Teezer."

"Is this the name you were given at birth?"

Her red lips went into a pout. "No."

"What name were you given at birth?"

"Kimberly."

"Kimberly—?"

"Kimberly Johnson."

"Thank you. Your occupation?"

"May I ask my lawyer a question?"

"Of course."

Listening to the murmurs from across the table, Carter picked up his pen and began to worry it between his index and middle fingers. He'd promised himself to stop doing that. He was doing better at his other promise—turn women off, not on. He'd done the best he could with Phoebe Angell, but he sensed trouble in his future. He was not going to use testosterone to settle this case, no matter how practical a solution it might—

"Services," Tammy Sue said sweetly. "Personal services."

"I already know from your answers to interrogatories that you have a career in personal services, Tammy Sue," Carter said. "I'd like you to tell me exactly what services you perform. Do you understand the question?"

Tammy Sue tilted her head up in thought. "Yes. I guess you could say I perform services that are personal in nature." She beamed at the cameraman.

"You need to be more specific," he said, getting frustrated. Why was she being so evasive?

"No, she doesn't," Phoebe answered for Tammy.

"Yes," Carter persisted, "she does. Are you a nurse,

Tammy Sue? A personal trainer? A housekeeper? A manicurist?"

"I object to the question," Phoebe said.

"Carter," Mallory said quietly, "perhaps we could refer to Tammy Sue as being in 'escort services' when we're speaking to the jury."

Duh. How slow could he be? "Fine," Carter said. He cleared his throat. "Place of residence? Or shall we slide past that one, too?"

"I live at 455 West Eighteenth Street." Tammy Sue answered this one proudly, but her chin began to tremble. "I hope I can go on living there. I used up most of my savings back in March and April when I couldn't work because of my hair."

If he had wondered why Phoebe Angell had chosen a prostitute as one of her prime witnesses, it was very clear now. He was no longer in the mood to laugh two hours later. He'd run through his list of neutral questions. Had she followed thc directions? Yes she had. To the letter. Had she worn latex gloves? The dye ran down into the gloves. Had she tested the dye on one strand of hair first? No, because she'd been using that Sensuous shade since she decided to go from blond to red and it had always worked before.

Now it was time for the big question. "So you weren't able to—solicit—any clients for what period of time? And what do you charge per—uh, service? And how many, um, services of this sort do you average per day?"

He hoped he looked cooler than he felt.

"I object strenuously to that question," Phoebe said.

"Ms. Angell, you know as well as I do that damages can't be assessed unless we know the income lost."

Phoebe looked at her client, then back at Carter. "We'll get back to you on that one."

"Okay. I reserve the right to re-depose this witness after you provide the information. Tammy Sue," he said at last, "I think that will do for now. Thank you for your cooperation. The rest of us—" and he included the court reporter and cameraman in his circling gaze "—should break for lunch."

When he and Mallory were alone, he said, "Don't you think more highly of me for not recognizing a prostitute when there's one right in front of me?"

To his surprise, she giggled. He wasn't sure if that was a good sign or a bad one.

6

MALLORY AND CARTER lunched on the sandwiches Phoebe had provided, because at one o'clock sharp they would depose Kevin Knightson, Phoebe Angell's original client.

The young man who entered the room was handsome and muscular. His flowing blond hair turned the lush green of spring leaves halfway down its length. He stepped through the door wearing a camera-ready smile, met Mallory's eyes, did a double take, slid his gaze toward Carter, opened his mouth to speak and then closed it again, looking like an actor in need of a prompt.

Phoebe, who'd ushered him in, gave him a sharp look and provided it. "Sit here," she said, pulling out the chair at the head of the table, and he did. Mallory noticed his mouth was twitching a little at the corners. Poor guy had stage fright.

"Is anything wrong?" Carter said.

"Oh, no," he said. "I just wasn't expecting such a, um, a big room. Or a cameraman. Or—" his gaze dropped to the table "—cookies." His voice was deep and sonorous, but it had a soft edge to it as well, and his statement ended on something very much like a giggle.

Yep, Mallory thought, *he's nervous.*

"Have one," Carter said, thrusting the plate toward

him. "Just relax," he went on, starting the spiel he'd given Tammy Sue and would probably give every witness—that we were all friends here and just trying to get at the truth. Then he said, "Coffee?"

"Please. Thank you. Much better than milk," their witness said incomprehensibly, then grabbed a napkin from the table, clamped it over his mouth and snorted into it. Recovered, he poured a large quantity of zero-calorie sweetener into the coffee Phoebe had put in front of him, added a larger quantity of heavy cream and stirred vigorously. Chewing a dainty bite of an oatmeal cookie, he glanced at Phoebe's puzzled face, arched his eyebrows at the cameraman, skimmed over Mallory and, at last, settled an appreciative gaze on Carter.

Carter broke the silence. "Can we begin now? Will you state your name for the court reporter, please."

"Kevin Knightson." Kevin smiled.

"Address?"

"Two-twenty-five East Sixty-seventh."

Mallory froze. The address had meant nothing to her when she studied the interrogatories, but it did now. It was Maybelle's address. Kevin Knightson couldn't be, could not possibly be, Richard's significant other of the green "tallywhacker."

What have I done to deserve this? Mallory began to draft a note in her head that she might pass to Carter. But what could she say without revealing that she had consulted an imagemaker? He'd think it was silly. Worse, he'd want to know why. Kevin didn't know her, so he couldn't give her away. Still, she wished she'd told Maybelle why she was in New York, and she'd do it this very evening.

Tread carefully, she might say in her note to Carter. *I*

have prior knowledge of this man. Yes, that's what she would say. She picked up her pen.

"Occupation?"

Kevin hesitated. "I'm an actor by profession." He smiled again and added, "You're supposed to say, 'Which restaurant?'"

Carter smiled back. "I know it's a tough business," he said, and Mallory heard real sympathy in his voice. "I wish you all the luck in the world. So—which restaurant?"

Everyone laughed except Mallory. She was busy writing her note.

"In March I was working for Blue Hill in Greenwich Village," Kevin said. "That ended when I showed up with green hair and eyebrows and fingernails. I put a temporary black dye on my hair and eyebrows," he said earnestly, "but it just turned them greenish black, and I couldn't do anything about my fingernails."

"Yes," Carter said thoughtfully. "And since that time, have you been employed?"

"Now and then," Kevin said, "doing this and that. Odd jobs for my landlady, behind-the-scenes work for an interior decorator and, um, seasonal work."

"Where are you employed now?"

"I object to that line of questioning," Phoebe said.

"About his job?" Carter couldn't hide his surprise.

"I can assure you he's engaged in nothing illegal or immoral," Phoebe said stubbornly.

"The defendants have a right to know his employment history in order to assess damages." Carter sounded just as stubborn.

Phoebe assumed a self-righteous air. "It's simply a job that requires a certain amount of anonymity. I'd appreciate it if you'd respect his privacy."

Carter sighed. "I guess I can do that, for the moment. However, I reserve the right to bring this witness to trial and cross-examine him in court."

"*Any*time," Kevin purred.

Mallory took this opportunity to slip her note to Carter. He read it, and his eyebrows drew together in a frown. He began to write rapidly, then nudged Mallory's legal pad back to her.

Mallory read what he'd written and gasped aloud. *You mean you've slept with him?* Observing that Phoebe, Kevin and the cameraman were all three staring at her, she said, "Sorry. My, it is a bit warm in here, isn't it?" She fanned herself with the legal pad.

No one answered. Apparently they didn't think so. While Carter went on to his next question, she wrote, *Of course I haven't slept with him!* She hit Carter sharply in the elbow with the corner of the pad, but he was busy interrogating.

"What was your income from acting prior to your decision to dye your hair red for the audition in question? Let me put it this way. What was your income last year?"

"Uh..." Kevin said. "There was the five hundred from the Boat Show, two-fifty from the Toy Fair...." He muttered away to himself for several minutes and finally announced a sum that wouldn't have covered Mallory's monthly mortgage payment.

"And what are you earning at your current job?"

"Um..." Kevin's eyes shifted away before he stammered out a number.

"So you're actually earning more now than you were before the alleged unfortunate incident with the dye?" Carter's staccato delivery made even Mallory flinch.

"But I might have gotten that part," Kevin insisted, "if I hadn't—"

Now Carter was both asking questions and writing on the pad. Apparently finished writing, he flicked the pad with his thumb and middle finger, propelling it with such force that it slid past Mallory and halfway down the polished table. The court reporter's clicking slowed. Phoebe's and Kevin's gazes followed the pad, and the cameraman appeared to be zooming in on it. Mallory retrieved it, her face heating up with both anger and embarrassment. But she couldn't keep herself from glancing down at the words Carter had written.

Then how do you know each other?

None of your business, she wrote, and shoved the pad an inch toward Carter.

Damned sure is. He's a witness in a case I have a vested interest in winning. Without a break in his questioning, Carter centered an elbow on the pad and slid it to his left.

Settling! she wrote below his elbow.

You hope!

"Perhaps this would be a good time for a break," Phoebe said acidly. "The two of you can discuss your problem verbally rather than by flying paper airplanes at each other."

"Fine," Carter said.

"Fine," Mallory said.

They glared at each other while Phoebe, Kevin, the cameraman and the court reporter retired, presumably, to restrooms and voice-mail messages.

"So?" Carter said, fire flashing from his eyes.

"It's a two-degrees-of-separation thing," Mallory said.

"What does that mean?"

"He doesn't know me. I know somebody who knows him, that's all. Information about him came up in an unrelated conversation. It's pure coincidence."

Carter stared at her for a long moment, then appeared to be calming down a little. "I wondered. He acted funny when he came in."

"There's no way he could know me," Mallory insisted. *Unless Richard mentioned my name to him, or Maybelle did. But that wouldn't be ethical of them, would it?* The telltale heat rose in her face again.

Carter was watching her closely. "Will knowing him keep you from doing your job right?"

"Of course not." *It just may keep me from getting my image right, that's all.*

"You're sure."

"Absolutely."

"Okay," he growled. "Guess I overreacted. Phoebe!" he yelled through the closed door. "We're ready to resume."

It occurred to Mallory that he must have grown up in a very large house, where the people he needed to talk to were at great distances from him. Someday she'd ask him.

DAMN IT, HE DIDN'T like Mallory having secrets. Mallory-type-people weren't supposed to have secrets. They were open, honest people, people you could depend on.

Depend on for what?

Well, for one hundred percent commitment to this case. For one hundred percent commitment to him, at least while they were working on this case. She wasn't supposed to be running around at night with God knew who to God knew where.

Of course, from her point of view it might look as if he were running around at night. But at least he'd told her who he was running around with. He wasn't keeping any secrets from her.

Well, one secret. That she was turning him on in a very unprofessional way and didn't even seem to be trying to.

He'd find out whom she was going out with. And how much she cared about him. He'd get started tonight. Damned if she was going to keep any secrets from him.

"NICE WEATHER," CARTER commented as they walked back to the hotel after wringing every last scrap of potential testimony out of Kevin Knightson.

"Very," Mallory said. The sky was inky and it was snowing, but Fifth Avenue was as bright as high noon with its vivid storefronts, lighted trees and glowing streetlamps. A huge, wet snowflake landed with a splat directly on her nose and melted at once. She started fishing for a tissue. Snow fell into her open handbag. The tissue was wet by the time she got it to her nose. Before she could use it, she slid sideways on the icy sidewalk. Carter, who'd been watching her futile exercise in nose-wiping, grabbed her around the shoulders.

For a second she stood absolutely still, leaning into him. It felt so warm. She felt so protected. She wanted to turn her face up to his and tempt him to lick the melted snowflake off her nose. She wished they could travel that way forever, through rain, snow, sleet and hail, over hills and deep into valleys, forge streams, swim rivers.

In that state of near-bliss, she did turn her face up to his, and what she said was, "I need snow boots."

Instead of licking the snowflake off her nose, he dropped his arm.

Her thudding heart seemed to drop to the pit of her stomach. One word—the *right* word—and he might have hugged her all the way back to the hotel. The hug might have led to a kiss—and then she wouldn't need Maybelle or the red jacket, wouldn't need anything, in fact, for the rest of her life except occasional room service. And a checkbook for keeping her bills paid promptly.

There I go again.

She was limp and sodden when they finally reached the suite. As they began to peel off dripping coats, scarves and gloves, she reflected that if this weather kept up, she would have to give up on black cashmere and switch to her microfiber trenchcoat that folded, like her robe, into one of its own pockets. Then she could buy a pair of those clear plastic shoes that Velcroed over her own shoes. No need to buy snow boots. She had sturdy, waterproof ones at home, and the plastic things were so cheap she could leave them behind when they left New York. As all these practical thoughts went through her mind, she was aware of the one thought that kept pushing itself to the forefront, that she desperately wished she had thought of something less practical to say to Carter.

"Do you have a date tonight?" he asked her in a sort of growly voice.

It was the first thing he'd said since she slipped on the ice and it startled her. "Uh, yes." In an hour, she'd be seeing Maybelle again, with a new awareness of how much help she actually needed.

"Are you going like that?"

She glanced down at the red jacket, the shell beneath it, her sedate knee-length skirt and heard, instead of her mother's voice, the voice of a devil whispering seductively to her. She smiled sweetly at Carter. "No, I was planning to freshen up a bit."

He seemed strangely relieved. "Here's your other jacket," he said, handing her the cleaning bag. "Freshen up and we can have a drink together before we go out. I have things to talk over with you—ah, things about the depositions today." He cleared his throat. "Several things."

"Thank you," she said. "I feel strung out enough to handle something strong. A margarita, that's what I want." She took a step, then another, and decided to experiment with letting her hips swing ever so slightly when she walked.

Did the Soft 'N' Comfy company realize how hard it was to swing your hips in their ever-so-comfortable shoes?

No! She would not give up her shoes for Carter!

But in the bedroom, she slowly unbuttoned the red jacket, slipped the black shell over her head and stood still for a moment, staring at herself in the mirror. Her bra was black, but it wasn't lacy. She had another bra with her. It was white—also not lacy. She slipped off the black bra.

Next she took a good hard look at her skirt. It was a very nice skirt, well cut and modestly knee-length even after she'd rolled the waistband over. She made another roll in the waistband, and another. Now the skirt showed quite a bit more leg and didn't bulge too badly at the waist. After staring at the black jacket in the cleaning bag, she slipped the red one on again, buttoned it and faced her reflection head-on.

"A-h-h-h," she squealed. "I can't do it."

"You okay?" Carter yelled from the sitting room.

For a man whose voice would carry from the president's Oval Office to the Executive Office Building, his hearing was amazing. "Fine," she called back, hearing her voice tremble a little. "Banged my elbow, that's all."

She removed her hands from her eyes. The top button of the jacket landed just below her breasts. The lapels curved down over them, almost covering them, but not quite. If she kept her shoulders hunched together...

But that wasn't the idea, was it. One millimeter at a time, she straightened her shoulders, feeling her breasts swell. This was how she'd go out into that sitting room, showing everything she had and proud of it.

A woman bent on seduction. That was the attitude she needed.

So that's what she was going to do, right after she brushed her teeth, freshened up her lipstick, lint-rolled her skirt, washed her bra and shell, shined up her shoes—

Never veer, never veer, never veer...

That was unmistakably Ellen Trent's voice, weakened, fading but still there. Mallory cursed under her breath. It wasn't as if she planned to give up everything she'd learned from her mother. She liked efficiency, cherished neatness. She was just going to relax the rigidity of it all and see if it made her come off a little softer, a little more feminine.

Hell. She brushed her teeth, put on lipstick and headed back to Carter.

When she stepped into the sitting room, he looked up, and she saw the stunned expression that crossed his face. Quickly he looked back down at the document he'd been reading. "You freshen up good," he muttered.

"Thank you." She perched on the edge of a chair and ever so slowly crossed her legs. "Would you rather have a drink here or in the bar downstairs?"

"Here. I've already ordered. I said to hurry."

"Good. I have to be somewhere at seven."

"Me, too. How long will it take you to get there?"

"I should leave here at a quarter to."

"Me, too."

"We're on the same schedule, then."

"Right. We have about thirty minutes to talk." He glanced at her again and shifted a little in the overstuffed, chintz-covered chair he was occupying. She leaned forward and gave him an encouraging smile. "So. What were your impressions of the witnesses today?" he said, and looked straight down the neckline of her jacket.

Get a grip, he growled at himself. *Get...a...frigging... grip! And not on her. No gripping her. No touching her. You're a lawyer, man. Act like one. She's your colleague. Treat her like one.*

I'm not letting her go out with anybody looking like that.

How're you going to stop her?

"Time is on our side," Mallory said, looking thoughtful and apparently not aware that her breasts were practically exploding out of her clothes. Wow, were they ever great breasts. She didn't have breasts when they were in law school. Couldn't have. He'd have noticed.

Flames stabbed him in the groin as he realized she wasn't wearing a bra, or if she was, it was the smallest, lowest-cut bra on the market. Damn. He could balance this brief on his erection. That would make a good impression.

He shifted his position again in a vain attempt to hide the clear evidence of what was really on his mind and said, "I agree. The slow pace of the law is playing to our advantage."

"Nobody got sick, the damage isn't permanent, not really, and the ordeal is almost over for the plaintiffs, at least in terms of their personal appearance."

"Yeah. Let's see." For something to do with his hands as well as something else to cover his lap, Carter reached for the printed calendar of events. "The dye incident happened on March 17. The lot went out on the twenty-fourth...it was on the shelves by the...right...the last bottle was purchased on the...and used a week later... So the person who bought that last bottle has had six months to grow out. If Kevin would cut off half his hair he'd be a blonde again."

He'd mentioned Kevin on purpose. He wanted to see her reaction. She got a little pink in the cheeks.

"Has Phoebe produced the pictures of her clients' hair yet?" she asked him.

"Nope. They're not due for another ten days."

"Can we get her to speed it up?"

"Probably not."

"We can try."

"You try."

"I will," Mallory said. "What about the other damages they're claiming?"

He answered her with half his brain. He really didn't think she was dating Kevin Knightson. He was as sure as he needed to be that Kevin was more interested in other men than in Mallory. So what was the connection?

"It's a shame we didn't succeed in negotiating with the plaintiffs back in the spring." She sighed, and Carter held his breath, waiting for her breasts to pop completely free from that sexy little jacket. "If we had, we might have managed to rehabilitate Tammy Sue. She might be selling cosmetics in a department store now."

"Your legal department negotiated just fine. Problem was that Phoebe got hold of them. Do we know how she did it?"

"The way I heard it," Mallory said, "she and her parents were at their country club in New Jersey talking to friends who knew somebody who knew somebody whose hair had turned green—you know how news spreads. Phoebe grasped the implications of a bit of gossip and zeroed in. She's a vulture," she concluded just as their drinks arrived.

A vulture *and* a black widow spider. Phoebe had slipped him her home phone number as they were leaving her offices. Once again, Carter faced the shameful possibility that he'd been given the case for just that reason, to seduce Phoebe into a settlement.

He took a sip of scotch. It went down smoothly, warming his throat. He could do it, seduce Phoebe into a settlement. Justice would be done. Sensuous was willing to make a fifty-million-dollar lump sum restitution to the plaintiffs. Phoebe would get fifty percent of that. Phoebe was asking for a hundred million. If the judge came even close to that, after years of filing appeals and generating their own enormous legal fees, it could bankrupt the company.

Carter looked at Mallory. She was chasing salt around the edge of her glass with the tip of a little pink tongue. Watching her was more warming than scotch. He thought about Phoebe, her spiky hair, her lipstick. Why did women wear gray lipstick? Did they think men were necrophiliacs?

Yes, he supposed he could seduce Phoebe, gray lipstick and all, but he wouldn't enjoy it and he'd hate himself. Nope, this one he was going to handle with his brain, and make sure Mallory noticed.

Mallory was sipping her drink and periodically checking her watch as she went on about the case. Should they push a little harder when they were reminding the witnesses of the settlement they might already have gotten? That's what she was saying when Carter cracked. He simply could not turn her loose in this town or, even worse, turn her over to the care of some man when she was showing her cleavage, wearing that skirt that displayed her thighs—oh, God, great thighs, too, slim but not skinny. Thighs to stroke. Thighs to slide between—

"Y'know," he said, feeling like a whirlpool of boiling hormones and trying to sound like the most dedicated, responsible lawyer ever to grace the bar, "we don't have any business going out tonight. Either of us. We ought to have a working dinner together. This is some good brainstorming we're doing here. I'm going to call Brie and tell her we'll make it another time." He looked expectantly at Mallory. Her turn. She looked surprised and ominously uncertain.

"I can't..."

He frowned at her.

"Well, I guess I can..." she amended herself.

His heart lightened. He lifted his eyebrows, silently telling her, "Go on, go on."

"Here's how it is," she said finally. "I'll have to break the date in person and then meet you for dinner. I should be able to make it by eight-fifteen. Want to order from room service or go out?"

"I'll see if I can get a reservation at the JUdson Grill. It's noisy enough that we'll be able to talk without anybody overhearing us." He picked up the phone and dialed Directory Assistance. He knew he couldn't spend the whole evening in the suite with her without jumping her. This was only Step One—don't let anybody else jump her. Step Two was win her respect for his intelligence and professional skill, which to him meant settling this case and effectively saving her company. His mouth watered just thinking about Step Three, when he'd make her desire his body, which had always been the easy part for him.

"Got the reservation," he yelled through the door when she withdrew to do who knew what before rushing out to taunt her date with her utter desirability—and then ditch the bastard.

"IT'S JUST A WORKING dinner," Mallory said breathlessly to Maybelle fifteen minutes later.

"Whoopee!" Maybelle cried. "Progress! Dickie!" And then to Mallory, "We gotta go shopping."

Mallory gasped. "I can't. I told Carter I'd be at the restaurant at eight-fifteen."

"So? I've gotta get back here at eight to meet with the president."

"The president?"

"Yes?" Richard said, gliding through the door.

"Get us our coats. Get the car. We're goin' to Bergdorf's."

"The president?" Mallory repeated.

"Uh-oh, a shopping spree," Dickie said, but was back in half a minute with Mallory's black cashmere and a coat for Maybelle that appeared to be several llamas sewn together.

She shrugged it on over a top that featured sequined diagonal stripes in purple, yellow and red. It made her look like a parrot. The llamas toned down the effect a bit. "Not our president," she said suddenly, as if Mallory's question had just registered. "He's the president of a little country, the kind they call 'emergin'.' Needs an image change if he's gonna win the next election. I shouldn'ta been blabbin' about it, either. Come on, hon, no time to waste."

"I don't need more clothes," Mallory protested as Maybelle dragged her to the car. It was an enormous pale blue Cadillac of indeterminate vintage, with Richard at the wheel.

"No, y'all jes' need more clothes like that little red jacket," Maybelle said. "Ain't no wonder he didn't want you seein' anybody else tonight."

Was that why he'd suggested the working dinner? "I have to admit he forced my hand and that's the only reason I wore the red jacket," Mallory said, and told Maybelle about the mustard shower.

Maybelle cackled. "Sounds like he wanted y'all out of that black jacket right bad."

"So I'll wear the red one again."

"Caint wear it ever' day or he'll catch on," Maybelle argued.

"Then I'll wear my black suit tomorrow whether he likes it or not."

Maybelle gave her a look.

"Okay," Mallory said, capitulating, "maybe I could buy another sexy jacket to wear tomorrow. But after that I really must leave to meet Carter."

"Id-zackly what I had in mind," Maybelle said smugly. "Jes' stick with me, hon, and you'll be at that restaurant right on time."

"MAYBELLE, WE HAVEN'T seen you in weeks," gushed a salesperson, rushing across a carpeted floor.

This was Bergdorf Goodman, as expensive a store as one could ever hope to avoid, and they were on the third floor—designer clothing. Yet the saleswoman was rushing toward a parrot wearing cowboy boots and shrouded in llamas. Mallory found her hospitality heartwarming.

Maybelle shrugged off the coat and dropped it on a bench as if she owned the place. "Haven't had a client who needed clothes in weeks. This one needs 'em bad and fast." Her tiny figure buzzed from one rack of clothing to another, a hummingbird now rather than a parrot.

"We need a coupla sexy suits—"

"I said one suit. I mean one jacket," Mallory puffed, pausing to zero in on a price tag and wipe her forehead. "I'll wear it with my black pants and skirt."

"Or some other black pants and skirt," Maybelle said.

"What I really need are some of those plastic shoes that go over your own shoes—"

"We'll find y'all some cute snow boots later," Maybelle said.

Mallory caught up to her in the Gianfranco Ferré in-store boutique and spoke to her in a hushed whisper.

"Maybelle, I do make a very nice salary, but I can't afford..."

Maybelle brushed off this absurd reasoning with a diamond-studded wave. "I have a charge account here," she said. "We can talk about the money later."

Mallory groaned. Later it would still be too much money.

Somehow she was in a dressing room, with Maybelle and the saleswoman ripping clothes off her and stuffing her into new ones.

"I think we can make it to the weekend without new undies," Maybelle confided in the saleswoman as if Mallory were not there. "Now, hon, that's what I call a black suit."

Mallory turned slowly to the mirror. This suit jacket had narrow shoulders, a fitted waist and was too short to cover even half her rear end. The pants were so narrow-legged that without the vents, she couldn't have gotten her bare feet through them.

She looked terrific in it. Even she had to admit it. She gritted her teeth. "Okay, I'll take the whole suit. But not another thing."

"Keep your new pants on," Maybelle said. "It'll save time."

In addition to the black suit, Mallory left the floor with a featherweight jacket that matched her eyes and a coordinating top, one skirt that wasn't as short as Phoebe Angell's but almost and another very curvy one in the new midcalf length. Both Maybelle and the saleslady, whose eyes had begun flashing dollar signs, insisted the longer skirt had to be worn with very high heels to achieve the proper proportions.

That's why they were speeding toward "Designer Shoes" on the fifth floor—to further reduce Mallory's stock and bond holdings she'd intended to live on in her retirement. Here the saleswoman began to confer with a salesman who'd been looking down his nose until he caught sight of Maybelle. In a dizzyingly short time, Mallory owned Prada pumps with sky-high heels.

"Do you have any of those plastic shoe covers—"

"Snow boots," Maybelle interrupted her. "We want a pair of them little high-heeled ones with the fur at the ankle. Don't wrap 'em. She'll wear 'em."

And once she was in them, Mallory realized she couldn't live without them. She'd stopped looking at price tags. Now was when she needed to live, not after she retired. It was a one-time binge. She'd never do it again. She'd have Maybelle paid off in two, three, four, ten years and start saving again.

Panic seized her. What was she thinking? Her mother would disown her.

Beside her, Maybelle said serenely, "I'll get the rest of this stuff brought right to your room in that suite. And I'll make sure your young man isn't there when they're delivered. Now you run on. You got twenty minutes, time to spare."

"I have to tell you something before I go."

"Shoot."

Mallory took a deep breath. "I'm a lawyer for Sensuous, the company that made the dye that turned Kevin's hair green. I started to tell you last night, but the subject changed somehow."

It was odd that Maybelle didn't seem surprised. She dismissed the confession Mallory had dreaded making with one of her dismissive waves. "Don't worry about it, hon." Her eyes widened, blue and innocent. "We're all perfessionals here. That's not gonna have nuthin' to do with the advice I have to give you."

"I would never have known if we hadn't deposed him today," Mallory said, surprisingly relieved that Maybelle didn't seem to be upset about the coincidence.

"And that wouldn't have been a problem if I hadn't shot my mouth off about him last night," Maybelle said, and sighed. "Don't know what made me do it. Then when he tole me y'all deposed him today, I—"

That startled Mallory. "He told you I deposed him?"

"*He* tole me he was bein' deposed," Maybelle said, again fixing Mallory with those innocent blue eyes. "*You* tole me it was you deposed him."

Too innocent, Mallory thought suddenly, and narrowed her own eyes.

"I think Kevvie's sorry he got snookered into this lawsuit," Maybelle went on. "If he hadn't, we coulda had that bathroom upstairs regrouted already—heck, I could have done the job myself—and Kevvie coulda had free haircuts and manicures until all the green was gone, at least where's you could see it." She snickered. "And he could be waitin' tables and auditioning again instead of...other stuff."

It was at that moment Mallory knew. It all came together, Kevin's peculiar behavior when he stepped into the conference room, his reluctance to reveal what his "seasonal" work was, the joke nobody understood about cookies and milk, the traditional snack children left for none other than—

"Maybelle," she croaked, "who was Santa Claus?"

Maybelle looked disgusted. "I never could keep a secret," she said. "Yep, hon, Kevin's yore Santy Claus."

7

CARTER STOOD AT the bar, not drinking, just leaning his elbow on it for support while he watched the door and ticked off the minutes, eight-twelve, eight-thirteen, eight-fourteen...

There she was, looking at the sign on the window, probably wondering why the JUdson Grill capitalized both the *J* and the *U* and wishing she were somewhere else besides here. She stepped in, and even as his pulse speeded up and his heart started directing all his blood south, he observed that she didn't look especially happy to see him. In fact, he had to say she was looking frantic.

"Hi," she said, looking at the room rather than at him. "Been waiting long?"

"Four minutes," he lied. He'd been there since eight, just in case the man she'd gone to see escorted her back to the restaurant, perhaps to see whom she was having dinner with. But she was alone. He examined her closely. "Our table's ready."

A very New York-looking woman, severely polished and self-assured, divested Mallory of her coat, and Carter steered her up to the headwaiter, another New York-looking woman who sent them off with a waiter—male, with a ponytail—to the table. Carter moved along behind Mallory. She was obviously upset. This was bad news. Her pants were the good news.

They weren't the loose-fitting, pleated ones she'd worn on the plane. These were so tight she'd have to call the fire department to help her get out of them. But what a lot of trouble to call the fire department when he'd be right there in the suite and happy to come to her rescue.

This delightful daydream faded when it occurred to him that she'd left the St. Regis wearing a skirt. What did a change in clothes indicate, a change of clothes that hadn't happened in the privacy of her bedroom?

They sat down. She leaned forward. Carter closed his eyes, and when he opened them, she was fiddling with the silverware. Her date must have given her a hard time, must have been mad that she wasn't going out with him, after all. So the man really liked her, or was really turned on by her, or both. Or maybe he was just a jerk with a bad temper, but Carter didn't think Mallory would go out with a jerk. So he liked her or was turned on by her and maybe she was turned on by him, too, and upset that Carter had sabotaged her plans for the evening. Damn. What had her plans for the evening been? Besides changing clothes.

The answer hit him in the stomach. The guy had ripped the skirt off her. She'd had to put on the pants, which she must keep in *his* apartment because Carter hadn't seen her in them before. Any fool could figure out what that meant.

The guy with the ponytail was back. "Would you like to start with a cocktail before dinner?"

"No," said Mallory.

"Menus?"

"Yes," Carter said.

"And a wine list?"

"You bet," Carter said.

He'd have to find out what her relationship was to this guy. Better to know. "You're all wound up about something," he said after he'd taken a cursory glance at the menu and another at the wine list. "I hope your date didn't go ballistic when you told him you had to work."

"Who?" She looked up from her menu. "Oh. No." At last she seemed actually to see him. "I was thinking you were all wound up about something. Was Brie mad?"

"She was okay about it," Carter said. In fact, Brie had said she needed to work, too, that stocks were down and bonds were up and she needed to strike while the iron was hot. Those were her actual words, and she'd added that she had some bonds she wanted to get him interested in.

"Is that Regis Philbin over there?" Mallory said next.

"It wouldn't surprise me," Carter said. "This is a media mogul hangout. Now, back to your date. If he didn't upset you, what did? Anything to do with *Santa Claus?*" He projected the words, noticing with satisfaction that she jumped, and with longing that her breasts undulated. The sudden emphasis on a couple of words was a technique he'd used in the courtroom, but it had never made anyone's breasts roll like that.

"What on earth do you mean?"

She was regaining her poise, but if he'd ever seen a guilty party he was seeing one now. "I mean," he said, "that you and Santa did a lot of whispering while he was holding you on his *lap*—" he projected that word, too "—and if a department store Santa came on to you, he should be reported."

"Are you crazy?" Openmouthed, she stared at him.

"Are you ready to order?" The waiter hovered

above them looking a lot like the referee in a boxing match. Carter realized his voice must have projected farther than he'd intended it to. He had to calm down before he got Regis Philbin's attention.

"Yes, we are," he said. "Mallory?"

She spoke to the waiter while still staring at him. "I'd like the pear and Roquefort salad and the sweetbreads."

He stared back. "I'll have the mussels and the steak. We'll share an order of your onion rings. And a bottle of..." He'd forgotten which wine and had to break eye contact to find it again on the list.

This couldn't be jealousy eating at him. He had no claim on Mallory. He felt responsible for her, though, a need to protect her from wolves and other predatory types.

Responsible for her in the big city. Yes, that was how he felt. "I just don't want anything unpleasant to happen to you," he said. "I made you go up there, and if he—"

"Made me go up where?"

"To sit on Santa's lap."

"Oh. There."

Where else? "So if he did anything like come on to you, or ask you out—"

"He didn't."

"Then does it have anything to do with that Kevin person?"

This time she didn't tell him he was crazy. Carter almost wished she had. Instead, she was pink with embarrassment and guiltier-looking than ever.

"Your wine, sir," said the wine steward, proffering the bottle for Carter's inspection.

"It's fine," he said without looking at it. "No, I don't want to taste it. Just pour it."

MALLORY HAD WALKED the distance from Bergdorf's to the restaurant hoping her sexy new snow boots would fail their first test. She'd slip on the icy sidewalk and fall down. As good as she was at not being noticed, she could lie there quietly on the cold concrete until she froze to death, which seemed infinitely preferable to telling Carter she'd sat on Kevin's lap and spilled out her soul to him.

She'd told the opposition's witness she wanted the lawyer for the defense for Christmas. Kevin could blackmail her. How far would she go to keep him from telling Carter how she felt about him? Worse, what if Kevin were, even now, telling Phoebe they had one of the defense lawyers in a bad spot? She groaned.

"Pardon?" Carter said, his eyebrows lifted.

"I'm dreading to tell you what I have to tell you." There. That was a start.

He seemed to tense up a little. "Always better to do it and get it over with."

She sighed. "It does have something to do with Kevin and with Santa Claus," she answered him.

"I knew it!"

Now they had everyone's attention. Even Regis Philbin looked up from the intense conversation going on at his table. "Carter," she said in an urgent whisper, "Kevin *was* Santa Claus."

His eyes widened. His mouth, which had been fixed in a thin line, began to quirk up at the corners. "That's his seasonal work?" Carter said. "Being a department store Santa Claus?" His smile broke through, followed by a snort of laughter.

Mallory fixed him with a stern glare. "I sat on the lap of a witness for the prosecution." While it was a great pleasure to see him smile, this was no laughing matter, and he didn't know the half of it, nor would he ever if she was lucky.

He stopped laughing almost as quickly as he had begun, and before her very eyes, Mallory could see the legal part of his mind kick in. "How do you know Kevin was Santa Claus?" His voice had cooled off.

Now she'd have to lie, which had been the best reason for not telling him anything. "I'd rather not tell you that." She set her jaw, knowing he wouldn't settle for that answer, but it would give her a second to think of another one.

"I'd rather you did." He set his jaw, too.

"A Roquefort-Pear Tower for the lady," their waiter droned above them. "Curried Mussels for you, sir, and an order of our famous onion rings."

Mallory could imagine the conversation going on in the kitchen. "Will you hurry up with the orders for that pair at table nineteen before they draw blood?"

She attacked her salad with feigned gusto, but even with her gaze downcast she could feel him boring a hole through her forehead.

"I guessed," she said suddenly.

"You guessed."

"Yes."

"How?"

"Oh, his voice. Or something."

"So this is just a guess on your part."

"No, then I asked."

"When did you ask him?"

"At a time when you...weren't there."

He frowned, probably trying to remember a point in

the afternoon that she and Kevin might have been alone, and she hoped he didn't put too much pressure on himself. He wasn't going to remember one because there hadn't been one.

"I see," he said at last. "Well, now that that's out of the way, maybe we can get back to work. How do you think we ought to handle the woman with green teeth we're deposing tomorrow?"

Carter figured he could talk and brood at the same time. He didn't believe she'd asked Kevin. He didn't think there'd been a time he'd been out of the room when she and Kevin were still in it. She was still keeping secrets from him. And if her dates last night and tonight hadn't been with Santa Claus or Kevin, because they were one and the same, they'd been with somebody or bodies else and who the hell was he or they?

Damn! It really mattered to him. That was the problem. The time wasn't right for their relationship to turn physical, but there she sat, so beautiful, so desirable with her marshmallow-cream breasts peeping out at him, her pale hair swinging and her eyes the color of a freezer pack looking so wide and innocent. He could have slept with this woman five years ago if he'd turned on his charm when he'd had a chance, and the fact that he hadn't grabbed at that chance was killing him.

He had to get her off his mind—although it wasn't his mind that was giving him a problem—until he'd successfully settled this case and she was swooning with admiration. So he'd take Brie out tomorrow night and somebody else Friday night and then figure out how to get through the weekend.

She was arguing with him even now, and he

couldn't blame her, because he'd been daydreaming and had said something stupid. No more stupidity. His life depended on it.

IT WAS THE FOLLOWING morning that Mallory felt the full impact of her recent veering—veering? careening!—from the beaten path to order and serenity.

By the time Carter came out of his room looking ready for breakfast—and a lot more coffee, judging from those bags under his eyes—she was dressed in her new tight pants, blue-green jacket, outrageous sheer tank top Maybelle had thrust into her bag at the last minute and high-heeled Pradas and was methodically dumping the entire contents of her handbag on the desk.

"What are you doing?"

"I can't find my credit card."

"Call and ask them to FedEx you another one."

She gave him a look that would have made her mother proud—until her mother saw her wearing aqua to the office.

"Okay," he muttered. "When did you use it last?"

She tried to focus on the lost card instead of on Carter's mouth. "Bloomingdale's, I think, when we went up to buy socks. You volunteered to handle our meals together and file for the reimbursement, so I think, yes, it must have been Bloomingdale's."

"You probably stuck it in some weird place."

"I never, as you put it, stick my credit card in some weird place. It has its place and that's where I put it."

"I might have known." She heard the sarcasm in his tone. "But this time—" he pointed a triumphant finger at her "—you didn't."

Her mouth tightened. "I hardly need you, who packed no socks, to point that out to me."

"No, I guess you don't. You never forget anything, right?" He moved closer to the desk, his gaze scanning the objects scattered over it. "Let's see what we've got here." His smile was not what you'd call friendly.

"Stay out of my handbag," she ordered him.

"I'm just looking for your credit card, not touching anything," he said. "A baggie full of first aid stuff isn't all that private, is it? Oh, my. Look what we've got here. A tiny tool kit. A tube of superglue. Do you have a foldaway crane in here somewhere? And where's the duct tape?"

Her face flamed with heat. She did, in fact, have small rolls of scotch tape and electrician's tape with her at all times, as well as a pair of scissors, two needles, one threaded with black and one with white, two small brass safety pins, self-sticking Velcro discs...

"It's good to be prepared in an emergency."

"How often do you have an emergency?" he asked, zeroing in on her sewing kit.

"I pull out a hem from time to time."

He raised his face to the ceiling. "Oh...my...God, it's a crisis. Throw that woman out of this meeting. Her hem's hanging."

"If you look your best, you work your best," Mallory said, but it sounded pretty lame even to her.

"Not necessarily," he said, suddenly shifting gears and becoming just Carter again, Carter without the attitude. "For example, I *look* great." He began helping her take things out of the handbag. When he ran onto the box that that held exactly twelve aspirin tablets, he opened it, shook four out into his hand and swallowed them dry. "And now I'm going to work better. Hey! Here's your credit card." He pulled it out of an inner pocket of the handbag and held it up triumphantly.

"Thank you," she said, feeling wilted. "I would never have looked for it there. That's my PalmPilot pocket, not my credit card pocket. No wonder I couldn't find it."

"I think it works out better never to know where anything is," he said as she repacked her handbag. "That way, when you lose it, you know you'll have to look everywhere for it."

"I see a flaw in your reasoning," she muttered.

"We can talk about it at breakfast," he said. "Ready to go? I'm going to have pancakes this morning. All those eggs are giving me too much energy."

I know a really great way you could use it up.

"GO ON INTO THE conference room," she said when they'd breakfasted and arrived at Angell and Angell. "I'm going to talk to Phoebe about speeding up the photographic evidence."

"Good luck," he muttered.

She left her briefcase in the hall outside the conference room door and stepped down to Phoebe's office, where she heard voices through the not-quite-closed door. Just one voice, actually, Phoebe's.

"I'm doing my best, Father," she was saying. "I don't like it, though. It's not ethical, and I—"

Mallory could just barely see Phoebe as she paced her office, a phone to her ear and her hand clasped to her forehead.

"I know," Phoebe said after a long listen. She sounded beaten.

"Yes, Father, I know. Tough and practical," she said a moment later. "I'll keep trying, of course."

Mallory slipped away. Alphonse Angell was controlling Phoebe's decisions from Minneapolis. She just wondered what he wanted his daughter to do that she considered unethical.

"Did she agree?" Carter asked when she returned to the conference room.

"I'll talk to her later," Mallory said. "She was busy."

"You chickened out." His eyes glittered devilishly.

"Did not!"

"Bet you did."

"If I did, may my teeth turn green," Mallory said, "and hush. Here's our witness."

"WHAT I DON'T UNNERSTAND," Maybelle said, "is why that woman don't just have her teeth whitened."

"What I don't understand," said the makeup artist, "is why she opened her mouth to the max and flung her head back in the middle of dyeing her hair."

Mallory stifled an impatient breath. She stifled it to keep from blowing the makeup artist in the eye. Maybelle had decreed they would meet at Bergdorf's at seven, and Mallory had arrived nearly in tears, wanting to tell Maybelle that in spite of the red jacket, pants she could hardly sit down in and flirty snow boots, nothing whatever had happened last night. In fact, the first thing Carter had done when they'd gotten home was call Brie and remake their date for tonight.

She had actually wept a little as she took the tags off her new clothes and hung them up, had wept for Carter and had wept at the money she'd spent. Or not spent, since she hadn't actually paid for them yet. And then, to top everything off, Carter had taken Phoebe Angell out to lunch.

Here she was in her darkest hour and all Maybelle could do was obsess on the woman with green teeth, that is, after telling Mallory her next step was to jazz up her makeup a little. So while Maybelle extolled the wonders of whitening, Mallory sat on a high stool at the Trish McEvoy counter in Bergdorf's Level of Beauty—a fancy name for a fancy basement—getting stuff brushed on her eyelids, her cheeks, her nose, along with a steady stream of instructions from a woman so elegant, so perfectly groomed that Mallory wondered how she ever got anything else done. Later, she'd get to spend a few hundred dollars more on makeup. Tonight, Maybelle had assured her, she wouldn't have to spend a dime, just had to sit still, be quiet and she'd have a whole new image in no time flat.

"I mean, those whitnin' jobs are incredible," Maybelle was saying now. "I talked the president into one."

The makeup artist came to a halt with the lip pencil. "The president?"

"Not ours," Mallory said, proud to be able to add something to this conversation. "The president of an emerging nation who needs to change his image to get reelected."

"Yay-yuh," Maybelle drawled. "And there was somethin' a little threat-nin' about these here teeth." She parted her lips to grasp tiny white incisors. "We had 'em filed down some. I told him if he looked less vicious he might act less vicious." And then she was right back to her obsession. "Course, I realize this woman you're talkin' about would be waitin' 'til after the trial—"

"There's not going to be a trial," Mallory cut in.

"Hold still," said the makeup artist.

"Course there's not gonna be a trial, but jes' supposin' there was a trial, she'd want to wait 'til after, but Kevin's tellin' me she says it's permanent."

"She has caps," Mallory said through closed lips. "That's the problem."

"But why'd she open her mouth and throw back her head?" the makeup artist persisted.

"Because," Mallory whistled through her teeth, "she was dyeing her hair red—"

"You can open your mouth now."

"—dyeing her hair red for the part of Annie Ado in a community theater production of *Oklahoma*, and she took a sudden notion to rehearse 'I Can't Say No.'"

"Thanks. I feel better knowing."

"What about the caps?" Maybelle was sticking to the topic.

"You can whiten teeth but you can't whiten porcelain caps," Mallory said.

"Way-ell, I'll be danged," Maybelle said. "Sure am glad the president has all his own teeth."

"There," said the makeup artist. "look at yourself."

Mallory had to admit the colors were subtle. The Be Prepared Pink kit had instantly struck a chord with her. The only thing she minded was that a lot of the kit had been transferred to her face, layered on top of moisturizer, concealer and brush-on foundation. She felt filled and frosted like a cake.

Buying them—she would hate that, too, when the time came to reimburse Maybelle. But her eyelashes were the worst blow. "People will think they're fake," she hissed to Maybelle, not wanting to hurt the makeup artist's feelings.

Maybelle sighed. "Oh, hon, you are nearly hopeless. You really are. But if you think I'm giving up on you, forget it. We're going to hit on something that makes you *feel* sexy, and that's all there is to it."

Mallory turned slowly to face her instead of the mirror. "What did you say?"

"Why, that's all this is about. You're as cute and feminine as you can be. I'm just lookin' for something that will make y'all *feel* that way."

"But I—"

"How'd y'all get to be like this anyhow?" Maybelle went from exasperated fellow-woman to counselor in a split second. "I don't usually get into the Freudian stuff, but I'm thinkin' in your case it might be intrestin' to know how you got your idea of what a woman was s'posed to be."

It stunned Mallory. Slowly she reached deep into her voluminous handbag, the handbag of an efficient woman who believes in Being Prepared. Carter had found her credit card before he'd gotten down to the bottom, where for some reason she'd been carrying her mother's latest book. In case she needed it, she supposed, and she needed it now. She pulled it out and thrust it at Maybelle.

"Read this," she said. "It will save us a world of time."

"Goody, bedtime readin'. Who wrote it?" Maybelle said, holding the book away from her, apparently to see it better.

"My mother."

"That should be intrestin'. Thanks, hon, I'll read it for sure. Here's your makeup." Although Mallory hadn't seen money or plastic change hands, the salesperson had produced a bag filled with makeup, which Maybelle handed to Mallory. "Go home and hit this guy with your new face. See what happens. Let's meet here again tomorrow night. We seem to be doin' better here than we do at the office." She frowned. "It may be them horns. The president looked a little scared when he saw 'em, too. Maybe I need me a less fancy desk."

And she was gone. She hadn't worn the llama coat tonight. The coat that was slowly receding up the escalator looked more like panda bears sewn together. Mallory watched until the last sliver of pansy-tooled boot vanished, then turned back to the makeup artist. "Don't I need to pay you for these?"

"Oh, no. It's taken care of."

"I can't let her go on buying things I'll have to pay for later," Mallory said, losing her natural need for discretion in the panic that set in. "I don't know the price of anything I've bought in the last two days. I could be bankrupt and not even realize it."

"Oh," the girl said, dismissing this idea with a wave of a perfect frosted-copper-tipped hand, "don't worry about it. Let Maybelle have her fun."

"I can't help liking her," Mallory said even more desperately, "but there's a limit to how much fun I can afford to let her have."

Now the girl actually laughed. "You may end up not paying for anything," she said.

"What?"

"You don't know about Maybelle, do you?"

"She has many, many diplomas," Mallory said grimly.

"She has many, many sections of Texas land, too," the girl said. "She inherited them when her husband died."

"How big's a section?"

"How would I know?" the girl said. "But it's a lot of acres, and some of them are right outside of town. In fact, they kind of sneak into the town. Pretty far into the town." Her grin was widening, and now she was just a cute, nice girl who was really, really good with makeup.

"Which town?"

"Dallas."

"Ah-h-h."

"Yeah, and the ones out in West Texas where Maybelle actually lived were so full of oil they weren't good for much else." She giggled.

"Oil," Mallory breathed out another "ah-h-h."

"I'm talking a lot of oil. Maybelle said it got 'right depressin' livin' with the smell.'" The girl laughed outright. "I told her that was the kind of depression I didn't need Wellbutrin for."

"So...I guess she has a charge account here, and she just..."

"The salespeople get a little orientation session on Maybelle when they start working at Bergdorf's," the girl said. "Maybelle takes, we add it up and send it up to bookkeeping, bookkeeping talks to her accountant and her accountant sends money. Everybody's happy."

Mallory was reduced to muttering inanities like, "I see. Uh-huh. Umm." She thanked the girl for the information and was pulling herself together to drift away when the girl said, "I put some instructions in the bag. I'm not sure you were paying attention while I was doing your face."

"Thank you," Mallory said. "I wasn't."

"Well, don't worry. Any problems, come back to me. I can fix the little stuff, Maybelle can fix the big stuff."

"You really think so?"

A mysterious expression settled over the girl's face. "I'll bet you a Pink Pearl lip gloss when that president she's counseling gets reelected."

8

FEEL SEXY. Mallory was still obsessing on the idea as she took the escalator up from the cosmetics level to the first floor. There she paused, thinking, making a plan. Until that magical moment she began to feel sexy inside, how was she going to make any headway with Carter? Maybe she needed a prop, just the way Carter needed that pen to worry between his fingers as if it were a cigarette. She walked slowly toward the front doors on Fifth Avenue, thinking what that prop might be, and remembered the mistletoe she'd admired on the Christmas floor at Bloomingdale's. Bergdorf's would surely have mistletoe, too.

Mallory found the elevators and went to the eighth floor, stepping out into another fantasy world of heavily decorated trees on which everything was for sale, trees and all. And there, hanging in a doorway, was a ball of mistletoe that was, if anything, bigger, greener—and more expensive—than the mistletoe at Bloomingdale's.

A few minutes later, she owned a ball of mistletoe. Seen from a different perspective, she owned something from Bergdorf's she'd actually paid for.

As soon as she stepped through the door of the suite, she discovered that she and Carter also owned a Christmas tree. It was a tiny, live tree in a beribboned terra-cotta pot, and someone had placed it on the small round table they could use for dining if they ever dined in. She assumed it was a special holiday courtesy of the St. Regis until she noticed the gift card.

"From a friend," it said. "May your Christmas wishes come true."

Probably one of Carter's women, she thought despondently. It smelled nice, though. Her mother's trees didn't smell at all. Nothing in her mother's house smelled of anything but bleach, ammonia or baking soda, the thrifty housewife's cleaning supplies. The Christmas tree, dutifully put up one week before Christmas and taken down on January 1, was, of course, fake.

She wondered what Maybelle would make of her mother's book. She'd know soon, because anything Maybelle thought was bound to come out of her mouth, and sooner rather than later.

With a sigh for what might have been, she lined up her new makeup on the marble counter in her bathroom and opened the mistletoe box. The ball of greenery came with its own little hanger, so she dragged a chair over to reach the archway that led to her bedroom door.

Then she hesitated, thought a minute, playing out the scene in her head. It would look too obvious if she backed him up toward her own bedroom door, so instead, she dragged the chair over to the arch that led to his bedroom door.

Who said she didn't need to travel with a tool kit? Newly grateful for her mother's wisdom, she went to work. It wasn't easy to install the hanger in the woodwork, and it was entirely possible the hotel would charge her for damages, but she reminded herself again that for the moment, money was no object.

It looked beautiful up there, and with the tree, the suite had taken on a wonderfully Christmassy air.

Now she could focus on the case until Carter came home. Assuming she could see through her eyelashes.

"INTEREST RATES ARE falling, the after-tax spread between munis, corporates and treasuries is narrowing dramatically and I personally feel this trend is going to continue."

"Uh-huh," Carter said. He was having sweetbreads tonight at a downtown restaurant—Chanterelle—because Mallory's sweetbreads had looked good the night before. These were the best he'd ever eaten. Brie's conversation, on the other hand, was not lighting his fire.

"We're expecting some very attractive new offerings from municipalities across the country. Highly rated, Carter, and in your tax bracket—" she frowned with apparent concern "—you really should be thinking of investing in them."

"Uh-huh." He was starting to wonder, as he had with Athena, what had made him think Brie might be the woman he'd want to settle down with. She was gorgeous as well as dedicated to her job, and serious, which was a fine quality in a long-term woman. He just hadn't remembered quite how serious. He speared the last bite of sweetbread. They were just great, the high point of the evening.

"I could make a call to your broker in the morning," Brie said. "In fact, I'd really like to establish a relationship with your brokerage firm. All their clients ought to get on this bandwagon fast."

"Hardy and White," Carter said.

"What?"

"Hardy and White, my brokerage firm in Chicago. Take them, they're yours." *If you'll let me go home.* "If you won't get mad when I tell you I have to eat and run. The case is starting to heat up. My workday's not over yet."

"I thought you were just taking depositions." Her eyes narrowed a bit. He guessed that was why he'd put her on his list of wife prospects. She'd shown an interest in the law.

"We are," he said as the waiter cleared plates away and proffered dessert menus. "But the evidence has revealed certain ramifications, potentially ruinous ramifications, that—"

"I'll have the crème brûlée and an espresso," Brie said briskly to the waiter.

"Same here," Carter said in a hurry, because her mouth was already poised for her next attack.

"Who should I ask for when I call Hardy and White?"

"Dan Whitcomb," Carter said. "Now, these ramifications have to be addressed before we find ourselves in a crisis situation with no way back to—"

"I'm sure you can find a minute in the morning to pave the way for me with Dan Whitcomb," Brie said, scribbling on her organizer screen.

"I'll do it first thing," Carter assured her earnestly. For a single phone call he could buy his soul back and go home to find out what Mallory had been up to tonight.

It seemed a small price to pay.

CARTER HADN'T WANTED to go to lunch with Phoebe Angell today, but she'd sort of cornered him. He hadn't enjoyed his date with Brie, either, but at least he'd had an excuse not to "pick up where we left off" with Phoebe, which was what she had suggested they do tonight. At her apartment. With take-out Chinese and a bottle of wine she described as "a big wine." Wasn't much doubt what she had in mind.

Both unsatisfactory events should have given him a chance to get Mallory and her secrets off his mind for a while, but they'd had just the opposite effect. She wasn't the same person he'd known in law school, and the change was upsetting. Chewing his lip, he stepped into the suite, where Mallory's eyelashes nearly knocked him back out.

"Hi," he said, practically stammering.

Sitting innocently at the desk working on her laptop, she batted those lashes once, twice. "Hi," she said. "Neither one of us seems to be much of a night owl."

"Not now, anyway. Pressures of work, stress..." He trailed off, fascinated by the smudgy line of blue-green under her eyes that he could see even through her lower lashes, which were just as stunning as the upper ones. Stunning in the sense that he felt stunned.

"Look on the table," she said next, making a few keystrokes. "Somebody sent you a Christmas tree."

He edged over to the tree and read the card. "I don't know who," he said. "Maybe somebody sent it to you." She had to know who sent it to her. One of the guys she'd been seeing, or worse, the one guy she'd gone out with all three nights they'd been in New York.

She seemed to be hesitating before she answered him, and when she did it wasn't a satisfactory, definitive answer at all. "Maybe," was all she said. "Anyway, we have a tree."

"Absolutely not," was what he'd been hoping she'd say.

"Merry Christmas," he said when he couldn't think of anything else. "I don't know about you, but my Christmas wish is to settle this case." *And win your undying admiration and feel man enough to court you and woo you…*

Again she wasn't saying anything, at least not very fast, so he edged back over to get another look at her eyelashes. "What are you working on?"

"I decided to do some research on porcelain caps."

"You don't need porcelain caps." Now he was nearly slobbering. In an effort to stop staring at her lashes—which were incredibly long and dark and curled up, so they cast spiky shadows on her cheeks in the most amazing way—he'd gotten a good look at the rest of her. She'd taken off the jacket she'd worn today, the one that matched her eyes, and now he was seeing her in those tight pants and the top she'd worn under it. You could almost but not quite see through it. He could almost but not quite see the shadow made by the curve of her breasts. Had she gone out with this guy, whoever he was, looking like she did now?

"Not caps for me," she said patiently. Swoop, swoop went her lashes. "How the plaintiff's witness could whiten her teeth to the color of her caps." Swoop, swoop.

"What did you find out?" He didn't give a damn. He just needed a distraction.

"Nothing."

"That's good." He was hypnotized by the difference in her appearance. Every line of her face seemed more—dramatic, or something.

"No, Carter, it isn't good." She turned to face him,

and her smile, a pinker, fuller smile than usual because her lower lip was pinker and fuller, had a patient look about it. "You must be tired. Maybe it's time for us to go to bed."

Oh, wow, do you really think so? You don't think we need to know each other better? Have a few kisses first? A romantic date or two?

Okay. If now is good for you, it's fine with me.

With a great deal of difficulty he pulled himself back from his Utopian dream. She hadn't meant go to bed *together*. She'd meant *separately*, she in her bed, he in his. Good thing he'd taken a second to think before he spoke.

She got up. "Of course, if you'd like to have a nightcap first, or some coffee..." She moved toward him. Instinctively he took a step back.

Her hair shone in the lamplight. It looked a little mussed, which worried him, because her hair was never mussed, but her lipstick was perfect, which reassured him. "Did we hear from Phoebe about the lineup for tomorrow?" What he really wanted to know was how long she'd been home.

"You just missed her call," Mallory said. She was moving her mouth differently, more slowly, shaping each word as she sent it through the slight smile that hovered around her mouth. "Supermom McGregor Ross got a baby-sitter so we're all set with our two witnesses." Her smile deepened. "Phoebe seemed disappointed not to find you here."

"In your imagination," Carter said. He hadn't dialed Phoebe's home phone number yet, and she'd mentioned his omission during lunch.

Mallory moved a little closer to him. "Not my imagination. You have a way about you."

He swallowed hard and backed up a step. She moved forward a step. They repeated this choreography a couple of times until he realized she'd nearly backed him up to his bedroom door. What was she doing? What was this all about?

She looked directly into his eyes. Her lips parted. "Look up," she said. "I've trapped you under the mistletoe."

"What mistle—" he got out, but the sudden pressure of Mallory's mouth cut off the word.

It was just a friendly kiss, a Christmas tradition, so why did it feel so hot? His entire being zinged with anticipation as he returned the kiss, still afraid to touch her without a sign that it was all right.

He felt her little gasp against his mouth. That was the sign he'd been waiting for. His blood went from room temperature to boiling in a second as he experienced a sudden vision of what she'd be like in bed. Shy at first, not, for once, taking the lead but not pretending to be unwilling either, and erupting under his touch into heat and flame, liquid gold pouring over him with burning intensity, coming fast and hard before he was inside her and after.

Sweat broke out on his forehead and his knees almost buckled as blood rushed to his rising erection. He placed a hand on each side of her face, held her there and let himself kiss her the way he'd been wanting to, deep and warm and hard. But he wanted more, the feel of her in his arms, and they went around her, his hands splayed across her back, crushing her breasts to his chest. Then he slid his hands down to her waist, pulling the delicious curves of her body into the hard tension of his.

Even that wasn't enough. He wanted to grasp that

curvy little bottom, pull her tighter, but as his hands began sliding even farther down her spine, a voice said, "What the hell are you doing?"

It wasn't Mallory's voice, it was the voice inside his head. She hadn't asked for this much from him, just a playful kiss under the mistletoe. Reluctantly, one small step at a time, he made himself let go of her.

She was pink, flushed, her mouth bruised-looking, her eyes heavy-lidded as she gazed up at him. Did he imagine it, or had her lips clung to his until the last possible moment? He'd imagined it. Those had been his lips clinging to hers. It wouldn't be like Mallory to cling, to urge him not to stop.

"Wow," she said. Her voice was husky. "Kiss Phoebe Angell like that once and we won't have any trouble talking her into settling."

Slowly, painfully, his hands dropped to his sides. Was she teasing him or did she mean it? Until she said it, he'd been very close to throwing caution to the winds and breaking his vow to earn her trust before he went for her body. But she had just put his greatest fear into words, that he'd been chosen to take this case because Phoebe Angell was a woman and he was a man women desired.

He stepped back, away from the mistletoe, away from the gaze coming at him from eyes he'd once thought of as icy and now saw as more like the inside of a sauna. "That's not really how you want me to settle this case, is it?"

He couldn't read the expression on her face as she whispered, "No, it isn't."

"Well, good, because it's not the way I want to settle it, either." He backed away into his own room and closed the door with a definite and firm click. It would have been...sophomoric to slam it.

Once in bed, hot and bothered, frustrated as all get out, he had a thought. He'd gone out with Athena and Brie and neither one of them had tried to jump him. He'd even imagined that Mallory had wanted him to go on kissing her—and more—but he'd been wrong. In fact, she'd suggested that he put the moves on Phoebe Angell.

He could come to only two conclusions. First, she didn't want him for herself. She just wanted him to settle this case by any means at his disposal. Second, he didn't have to worry about turning off his charm because he'd already lost it. Twenty-nine years old and the testosterone leak had finally done its job. He'd run out.

No, he couldn't have run out, not as aroused as he was. He still had some left, just not enough to leak. If he was no longer a sex god—not the way he thought about himself, but the way many a woman had described him—and he wasn't smart enough to impress Mallory with his brains, then what the hell was he?

Of course, there was still, as Mallory had said, Phoebe Angell. She *did* seem to be under the spell of his charms.

The very thought made for a sadly sleepless night.

MALLORY COULDN'T SLEEP. At last she got up, put on her packable, practical travel robe, which she suddenly hated, and tiptoed out into the sitting room. There was hot chocolate mix in the little kitchen. She'd make a cup, see if it put her to sleep.

From where she stood, she could see through the arch with the mistletoe over it, down the little jog straight to Carter's door. She couldn't resist. Her feet went toward that door. Carefully she placed her ear against it. From inside came the soft, rumbling snore she'd imagined in her fantasy of him, the snore that would vibrate her naked skin, puff against her ear, soft and comforting. A snore to sleep to.

The ache between her thighs grew almost unbearable. Now she was letting the door hold her up as she sank against it, wanting him with an intensity she didn't think she was capable of. The door opened and, with a shriek, she fell into his room.

The light went on. He sat up in bed, blinking sleepily. "Mallory?" he said, squinting at her.

"Uh, yes," Mallory quavered, scrambling up off the floor. "Gosh, I'm so sorry. I couldn't sleep, so I got up to make myself some cocoa, and I—"

He's naked under that sheet.

And his room's a mess.

"And I tripped over the footstool, you know, the little one that sits in front of that beige velvet chair," she babbled on, making up the lie as she went along. "I was afraid it might have awakened you, so I listened at the door to make sure you were still asleep."

He was waking up now. She could tell. He was staring at her with the strangest look on his face even as he pulled the sheet a little farther up his chest.

It was probably her robe. He hated it even more than she did. And it didn't make her feel the least bit sexy.

"Then the door opened all by itself and I fell in and I'm so, so sorry, so go right back to sleep because it won't happen again."

There. She'd gotten out alive. Having humiliated herself again, she darted into her room, closed the door and just stood there a minute, shaking. One minute more and she'd have climbed into bed with him. Or cleaned up his room.

No, she would definitely have climbed into bed with him.

In fact, if she wanted to get anywhere with him, that that was what she would have to do. She'd discuss it with Maybelle tomorrow night.

THAT HAD BEEN A NEAR MISS. Carter was still thinking about it as he stood in the shower the next morning trying to cool down. She'd been right there within reach—well, she'd been within reach plenty of times before, but this time he'd really had to fight to keep from dragging her into his bed. He'd been ready for her, hot and drowsy and drugged with desire that had been building so fast inside him he could hardly keep himself under control.

But she wouldn't have respected him for taking advantage of her, would she? She'd have been sorry she'd awakened him. After all, the whole episode had been due to happenstance. It's not like she'd wanted to fall into his room.

He growled, got out of the shower and toweled himself off. One more happenstance was going to break him. On top of that, today he would have to depose a woman whose baby girl had been sleeping peacefully in some kind of baby chair that was safely—safely, mind you—resting on the bathroom counter while she refreshed—*refreshed,* the brief said—her *natural* hair color. When she looked up into the mirror and saw her hair turning green she'd flung out her hands, and by the time she'd calmed down, her baby had green spots on her chest. A precious little baby girl, could have been a baby model, but couldn't because she had green spots on her chest.

Not anymore, of course. But back in April it had been a tragedy she didn't think the family would ever get over.

Bull.

There was so much he had to do at once. He had to settle this case, impress Mallory, make her want to make love with a man as smart and successful as he was.

What he had to do was make her think he was smart and successful, whether he settled the case or won it or neither. He dressed quickly before he chewed his lower lip off completely and went out into the sitting room.

As always, Mallory was already there, looking more rattled than she had yesterday morning when she couldn't find her credit card. She was wearing her black suit. He took another look. It wasn't her black suit, it was another, completely different black suit. It was possible she wasn't even wearing one of those tops she called shells, just the tight-fitting suit jacket and those skinny pants.

She was irresistible.

But he had to resist. He needed to distract himself. His eyes darted around the room. "Lose something else?" he said.

"No, no, well, I was looking for the card someone gave me, a hairdresser she knows here, because I'm going to need a cut if we're here much longer or I'll look like a throwback to the seventies, and I just wanted to be prepared, you know, make an appointment and then cancel if we go home before—"

She was tossing business cards like a madwoman.

Suddenly she scooped them all up again in her hand and said, "The truth is, I'm just so embarrassed about last night. I feel really stupid."

Carter had a brainstorm. For once in his life, he would behave like a true gentleman. "What happened last night?" he said, hoping the expression on his face was a puzzled one.

"You don't remember?" She stopped shuffling cards.

"Last night. Sure I remember last night. I came in, you were online doing a Google on porcelain caps, we got a tree and you kissed me under the mistletoe."

She blushed. "I was overcome with Christmas spirit. But after that, you don't remember anything after that?"

"Yeah, I remember after that."

She got even redder. "What do you remember?"

"Seven o'clock this morning."

She stared at him. "But you spoke to me."

"I always speak to you. What are you talking about?"

"Nothing," she said, and her smile was faint but very pretty. "I guess we're ready to go down to breakfast."

While her eyelashes didn't look quite as long this morning, they were still a lot longer than they'd been yesterday and he didn't want to start obsessing on them or thinking about his near miss last night, so he got behind her and started herding her toward the door, not letting himself stare at her butt this time.

They were nearly out the door when he had another brainstorm. It would be a small thing, but it might ring one of her bells. After all, she'd brought home mistletoe to remind them of the season. "Uh-oh, forgot something," he said. "You go ahead. Get a table. I'll be on the next elevator," and he shoved her out the door and closed it.

It took him three minutes to find what he was looking for beneath the mound composed of every garment he'd put on and taken off since they arrived, and the only reason it was one mound was that the housekeeper had tried to restore some order to the room as well as cleaning it. But five minutes later the Christmas tree bore a single ornament, the one he'd bought at Bloomingdale's as his contribution to the grab bag at the office Christmas party. It was a huge handblown glass ball with gold and silver swirled around it. It dwarfed the tiny tree, but he thought it looked pretty nice. He hoped Mallory would notice it.

On the way to the elevator he saw a card lying on the floor of the hallway. Instinctively, he bent down to pick it up. And because he had to wait a couple of minutes for the elevator, he read it.

"M. Ewing. ImageMakers. A new you in—"

In no time flat?

The imagemaker could use a new ad agency. But then the concept sank in. Image. His image. The image he wanted to change.

People like these tended to be quacks.

He guessed some weren't. Important public figures paid big money for the services of imagemakers.

He'd never know if this one was legitimate or quack. He didn't need anybody to help him. He just needed to—

Or maybe he did. Need help. Wouldn't hurt to keep the card around. The elevator arrived. He put the card in his pocket and went downstairs to have breakfast with Mallory, and this morning he was going back to eggs. To hell with his heart. He needed all the energy he could get.

9

"DID THE GREEN SPOTS give the baby any discomfort?"

"No, no thanks to your hair dye," McGregor Ross huffed. Carter worried the fountain pen between his index and middle fingers. He thought she might be a very pretty woman without that shrewish expression on her face. "I wiped the dye off immediately and put lotion on her chest."

"How long did the spots persist?"

"Long enough for her to miss out on a very important audition, one that might have launched her modeling career."

"But she's able to make auditions now." Carter smiled encouragingly.

"She's growing up! She's lost six crucial months of opportunity!"

"Did she have any assignments in the months before the dye incident?"

"No, but..." Mrs. Ross ruffled like an angry chicken.

"Did she have assignments after the green spots went away?"

"Well, no, but..."

"I object to this line of questioning," Phoebe broke in.

He needed a break, a break from the avaricious Ms. Ross, a break from Phoebe's come-hither eyes and the way they contrasted with her sharp comments and objections, and most of all a break from the pressure of Mallory sitting beside him, so close he could almost feel the heat of their bodies combining in an explosive chemical reaction.

He got his chance in the form of a telephone call. Excusing himself, he followed the paralegal who'd brought the message and picked up the phone in an empty office.

"Carter. Bill Decker."

"Hey. Bill. What's up?" Between them, he and Mallory had checked in with the boss three times a day, so Bill must have had an idea good enough that he couldn't wait to hear from one of them.

"I've been thinking." And he came to a halt.

"Thinking..." Carter said, using the same encouraging tone he'd used on McGregor Ross.

"Well, I sort of hate to bring it up."

Carter controlled his impatience. It was quiet in the empty room, no greedy moms, no Phoebe, no Mallory. Of course, he had no idea what they were up to in the conference room, and he really should get back.

"How are you and Phoebe Angell getting along?"

That brought back his focus. "Fine, I think. Did she complain about something I said or did?"

"No, no." Bill sounded as if his mind was off on another tangent. "Well, just that she inquired about what sort of relationship you had with Mallory, and I wondered..."

Now Carter just waited. He had a bad feeling he knew what was coming.

"I assured her that you and Mallory were merely colleagues, I mean, Mallory is *Mallory.*"

Not anymore. Carter ground his pen between his fingers. Without considering the alternatives, Bill was dismissing any possibility that he might have a physical interest in Mallory. "My relationship to Mallory is none of Phoebe's business," he said, sounding as uptight as he felt.

"Of course not," Bill said quickly, "but..."

Carter sighed. "But what, Bill? Spit it out."

"I was just wondering if a little personal attention to Phoebe might pave the way, soften the atmosphere, rechannel her interests. You understand what I'm saying?"

How could I not understand? You explained it three ways.

"Is that why you put me on the case?" he asked. It was blunt and not the right thing to say to a man who was, at the moment, his boss, but he had to know. "You want me to prostitute myself to get Sensuous off the hook?"

"Of course not." Bill sounded so shocked that it confirmed Carter's suspicion that it was, in fact, precisely why he'd gotten this case. Then Bill went on, sounding smooth as tofu, "I wanted you on this case because I felt sure you could bring it to settlement—" he hesitated "—using all the means at your disposal."

There it was, the challenge, out in the open. "I feel just as sure I can reach settlement, Bill," Carter said, deciding that outrage wouldn't do him any good. "I'd prefer to handle it in a more straightforward way, though."

"Have you come up with a straightforward idea?" Bill's tone was dry.

"Mallory and I are full of ideas," Carter lied. "It's only a matter of choosing the one that will work best."

They ended the call on good terms, but Carter wasn't on good terms with himself. That call had been the straw that broke the camel's back. For the last five minutes he'd been fingering the ImageMakers card in his pocket and now he pulled it out. He needed to change his image—not merely to qualify for Mallory, but to approve of himself. He'd use a fake name, pay cash, no one would ever know that the up-and-coming Carter Compton was, at the ripe old age of twenty-nine, having a crisis of confidence.

A male voice answered the ImageMakers number. "I'd like to make an appointment," Carter said.

"Yes," the voice purred. "Your name?"

Carter hesitated. "Jack Wright."

"Mr. Wright."

I'd like to be. Was that what this was all about? Being Mallory's Mr. Right?

As that thought shot through his head it startled him so badly he dropped his pen and was about to grind it out under his shoe before he remembered it was a Mont Blanc pen and not a lighted cigarette.

He bent his knees to pick it up. "Um, maybe this isn't such a good idea," he muttered, feeling perspiration pop out on his forehead.

"When our clients say that," said the voice, "it usually indicates an emergency. Can you come in right now?"

"Right now?" He actually squeaked the words. "No, no, I can't. I'm working."

"Lunch hour?"

Just as he'd thought. A quack. No clients. Not even enough sophistication to pretend that M. Ewing was very busy but perhaps they could sneak him in somewhere. But he was starting to think it might be an emergency, just like the man said, and he'd never get an appointment with a psychiatrist this fast. Maybe he just needed somebody to talk to and almost anybody would do.

"I could make it by twelve-thirty," he said slowly.

"She'll see you then."

She? "She?" he said aloud.

The voice turned frosty. "You have a problem consulting a woman about your image?"

"No, no, no," he hastened to say, feeling his current image slipping right down through all twenty-four floors of the building that lay beneath his feet. "I just, you know, with the name 'M. Ewing' I thought..." He pulled himself together. "I'll be there at twelve-thirty," he said, using a firm tone of voice and knowing he needed someone to use a firm hand on him in this situation. It was time for Carter Compton, the talker, the negotiator, the one always in the lead, to do some listening.

First he had to listen to a woman who was determined to thrust her infant daughter into the modeling game. Poor kid.

At twelve twenty-five, having left Mallory and Phoebe back at the law offices staring oddly at him when he deserted them, he gazed with grudging approval at the mansion which apparently lodged ImageMakers. This place would sell for three or four times the value of his parents' house in suburban Chicago, but it was less flagrantly ostentatious. He liked that.

He went up the cleanly shoveled sidewalk to the front door, where his positive feelings took a rapid downturn. He stared at the doorknocker. No way was he picking up that thing and banging it on its balls. It gave him a cramp in the groin just to think about it. So he knocked with his knuckles. A moment later the door opened.

"Mr. Wright," the man at the door said, but his eyes went directly to the doorknocker. "Oh, thank goodness, I thought it had been stolen."

"Ever think of getting a doorbell?" Carter growled.

The man smiled. "I'm Richard," he said. "Maybelle's ready to see you."

"Maybelle?" Carter said, but followed him across the marble foyer, anyway. He took in the office of this Maybelle person in one swift scan, observed that it was unusual, then gave the woman behind the nonstandard desk a once-over and decided her hair must have gone through repeated shock treatment. He sat down, glared at her and said, "Your knocker is obscene. You being interested in other people's images, I'm surprised you're not more careful about your own."

The woman had been looking him over, too, but now she narrowed her focus to his face. "What y'all talkin' about?"

Carter winced just hearing her voice. A quack all right, and he was getting out of here just as soon as he made his point about the knocker.

"The doorknocker," he said.

"Oh, that. I tole Dickie to pick one out. I don't never use the front door, so I don't know what he got. You don't like it? It sure bangs good."

He stood up. "You'd better take a look at it, decide for yourself."

If she said, "Hey, that's awesome," or whatever she'd say in that Texas accent of hers, he'd know he had no business being here. Instead, as they stepped outside together and she got a look at the door, she screamed, "Dickie."

The scream echoed off the elegant facades that lined the quiet, winterbound street. "Ma'am?" Richard appeared, wearing a sheepish expression.

"What is that?" Maybelle pointed with a shaking finger.

"Well, it's a—"

"Don't say it," Maybelle snapped. "You tryin' to ruin me? What are people gonna think? I'll tell you what—that I'm runnin' a male-escort service here."

Dickie drew himself up to his full, extremely muscular height. "To me, it said 'We have a sense of *humor* here.'"

"Way-ell, that ain't what it says to me. Get rid of it. Get me some nice antique thing that don't look like nuthin' but a doorknocker, you hear?"

"Okay," Dickie, or Richard, said with a long-suffering sigh.

"And make us some coffee. You like regular or deecaf." She turned an assessing gaze on Carter, who was getting pretty cold out there on the stoop, while this skinny little woman in blue jeans and a T-shirt with a panther printed on it didn't seem to notice.

"Regular, but I don't—" He was leaving, was what he'd decided, just as soon as he got his overcoat back.

The gaze turned approving. "I'll be danged. He likes regular. Y'all hear that, Dickie? Brew us up a pot of real strong stuff." She turned to Carter, and her expression turned wistful. "Y'all don't happen to like it percolated, do you? Kindly muddy like?"

"No, but you have what you like, because I—"

"He don't," Maybelle told Dickie. "So drip it. Nobody's perfect," she added before she marched Carter back across the foyer. He had his mouth open to ask for his coat when she said, "That's not all you come here for, was it? To yell at me about the doorknocker?"

Instead of asking for his coat, he looked at her, looked into big blue eyes that offered to listen to whatever he had to say. "No," he admitted. "The doorknocker thing was a sidebar."

"Then sit down," she said, marching toward the chair behind the desk that looked like the fossilized nest of some long-gone pterodactyl.

"Now that we've done the doorknob," she said, "tell me what y'all think of this here desk. Mebbe I'd better take a minute to work on my own image."

SHE'D DONE EVERYTHING Maybelle had told her to do and still he'd taken somebody else out to lunch. It wasn't Phoebe Angell, either. At least Phoebe was a known quantity.

She'd refused Phoebe's halfhearted invitation to have lunch. The woman's expression had said, "I'd rather be a waitress on roller skates than have lunch with you." Instead, she went back to the hotel, netted a table for one in the restaurant, ordered a salad and darted up to the suite. She needed to take a look at herself in the full-length mirror, figure out what she might have done wrong.

She flung open the door of the room, and the first thing she saw was the tiny Christmas tree—wearing the ornament Carter had bought at Bloomingdale's their first night here.

The nonverbal message in that single ornament stunned her. She was too verbal to know what it meant, but she was certain it was meant to tell her something. "Glad you bought the mistletoe"—something like that. She became aware of the heavy weight that had settled in the lower half of her body, realizing it was nothing new, it was there every second she was with Carter, but it seemed to be getting heavier, harder to ignore.

While she gazed at the ornament, a certainty settled in her bones. *Tonight or never.*

CARTER CAME BACK TO Phoebe's conference room looking like raw skin. Shaken and vulnerable, those were the words that came to Mallory's mind. Also, he was late.

"Are you all right?" she said, then realized she'd looked at her watch. Scolding him about his lateness was hardly the path to seduction.

"Is anyone all right after a root canal?" he growled.

"Oh, sorry," she said lamely. He hadn't complained of a toothache. She hadn't noticed any swelling. He'd had crunchy bacon with his breakfast. It must have come on quite suddenly.

Or he was lying.

Apparently he wasn't feeling too bad, because he wound up the session with McGregor Ross at five-thirty promptly, and then said he had to leave.

At that point, she hoped it *was* a dentist he was running off to. Her resolve flagged as she stomped her way through a light snow to the hotel, her new snow boots the only bright spot in her cloudy sky. How could she ever have thought of wearing plastic thingies over her Soft 'N' Comfys?

With a desolate hour to spare before meeting Maybelle at Bergdorf's, she decided to check her e-mail.

It surprised her so much to see Macon's address in the Sender column that she ignored all her business messages and opened his. It was perfunctory as usual, but the message was not at all usual.

"mallory do you think anybody brought up like we were can relax enough to fall in love macon"

Macon? Asking about love? Was the earth still turning? Had the moon escaped?

She wrote back, "I don't know, but I think we have to give it a try to find out." Her fingers slowed on the keyboard, then she typed rapidly, "What exactly is it that you're doing in Pennsylvania?"

She got up from the computer. The suite seemed empty without Carter. She felt as if her life had been empty without Carter, would continue to be empty without him. That was pretty good advice she'd given Macon, now that she thought about it. She'd never know until she gave it a try.

"Tonight we go for underwear," she informed Maybelle when they met in Bergdorf's first floor Fine Jewelry. She looked her imagemaker straight in the eye.

"Oh, hon, this is startin' to sound good," Maybelle crooned. "I was thinkin' fingernails with stars on 'em tonight and save the underwear for the weekend, but if you're ready, let's go for it. Anything intrestin' happen today?"

They started up the escalator toward Lingerie. "Carter's out with somebody," Mallory said, feeling despondent. "Not Phoebe, and he didn't mention Athena or Brie, so this one's an entirely new challenge." She could bet her name began with a *C*, unless the *C*s were all unavailable. "He might even have taken her out to lunch," she told Maybelle. "He said he'd had a root canal. He might have been lying, but he did look awful when he came back."

Maybelle let out a bark of laughter. "I consulted with

a man today who acted like tawkin' to me was worse than havin' a root canal," she said, shaking her head.

"Men," Mallory said. "They just hate opening up, don't they?"

"Yep, jes' like oysters," Maybelle said. Her eyes gleamed with victory. "I knew jes' by lookin' at this one that pryin' wouldn't do no good. I had to smash his shell with a sledge hammer. I made him come back a second time in the same day. That's a record."

Mallory felt a certain sympathy for the guy. "What was his problem, since we're not mentioning names?" she asked.

"Oh, one of the old standards," Maybelle said offhandedly. "He's always had a way with the ladies, but now he wants 'em to look at him in a different way. If you ask me, he's in love with one gal and don't know it yet, and even if he did know it, he wouldn't have no idea how to tell her."

Turned around backward, that could describe me. But they'd arrived in lingerie, and Maybelle vanished into the foam of silk and nylon, pastels, blacks and leopard prints. While she circled, grabbing things up, chatting with yet another obsequious salesperson, Mallory stood transfixed, staring at a mannequin in a hot-pink gown and robe. The robe was kimono-style with wide, flowing sleeves and a sash. It was short, and the gown was shorter, lace-trimmed, a simple shift with spaghetti straps.

Maybelle zoomed by toward a dressing room. "I want this," Mallory said.

Maybelle screeched to a halt. "That's real purty." She said to the salesperson. "Get her one to try on, will you, hon?"

In the dressing room Mallory reached first for the

hot pink ensemble. She had a feeling about it, pure intuition, and the feeling intensified when she stepped into the tiny gown. She was naked beneath it, and it brushed her body like a caress. She wriggled with pleasure. The familiar ache of wanting deepened until she thought her knees might buckle under her. If Carter had been in the dressing room with her—

She'd better try the robe. She put it on, wrapped it across her breasts, tied it, then watched it begin to part in the front, silk sliding against silk. For a moment she leaned against the dressing room wall.

"You doin' okay in there?" Maybelle screeched.

"Yes." She whispered the word.

"Huh?"

"I finally know what you mean," she said just loudly enough to carry through the door. "Now I feel sexy."

"Whatever she's got on," she heard Maybelle hiss to the saleslady, "we'll take it." Then her voice came faintly through the closed door. "Now that you feel it, hon, what're you gonna do about it?"

It felt a lot like how going to confession must feel. In the anonymity of the dressing room, speaking softly through the door, Mallory told Maybelle exactly what she intended to do.

When she got home with her treasure, lacy bras and panties, the pink robe and gown and several more equally sheer and arousing sleep outfits, she realized she hadn't asked Maybelle if she'd started reading her mother's book.

Her mother—and her books—were way down on her list of priorities right now. What was on her mind was that it was only eight-twenty and Carter was at home. She could tell he was at home because his overcoat lay on one chair and his tie on another, his briefcase was open and the contents spread out over the table that held the Christmas tree. A lot of Carter was there to look at, just not Carter himself. He had to be in his bedroom.

Alone, she hoped.

She didn't hear any giggling female voices or see any evidence of a woman, no stiletto heels kicked into a corner, no feminine-looking coat or handbag. Whatever he'd done tonight must have ended in complete disaster. She tried to feel sorry, but it wasn't easy.

She tiptoed into her own room with her new unmentionables, then tiptoed back out. She couldn't help herself—she had to hang up that overcoat. Once she'd done that, she had to lay the tie out in a neat fold on the little table behind the mistletoe-hung arch, and once she'd done that, she had to put his papers into squared-off stacks.

Now she could put her own things away. Suddenly starving, she went to her bedroom and ordered from room service. "Shall we deliver your dinner with Mr. Compton's?" said the voice that answered the phone.

"One dinner or two?" she wanted to ask, but couldn't. She thought about it for a minute. "No, bring his when it's ready."

It was a little like a French farce. From her bedroom, she heard the bell ring, then heard Carter tiptoe out to receive his room service order. Mallory had her ear glued to the door. It sounded as if the waiter was setting up in his bedroom. So when the bell rang a second time thirty minutes later, she tiptoed out and steered the waiter with his cart into her room. As the waiter left her room, she heard Carter tiptoe out with his empty tray.

She felt the tension building. When she did what she

intended to do, she might actually surprise him into compliance. Her plan was what you might call an ambush, very unsportsman-like, but highly effective.

The evening wore on. Mallory ate dinner and did another tiptoeing act to deposit the tray outside the door of the suite. From Carter's room came the muted sounds of an action movie—bam! bang! crash! kerplooey! Next she took a long, soaking bubble bath. She washed her hair, blow-dried it to a smooth, silky fall, redid her makeup. She found herself drawn to the stock market channel and made herself switch to a romantic movie.

At last she couldn't stand it anymore and tiptoed over to listen at Carter's door. He was asleep. The soft, rumbling snore was a sure sign.

It was time.

As if it were a battle campaign, she checked her ammunition one last time. Makeup, not too much, not too little, her hair, the hang of the hot-pink gown and robe, her fingernails and toenails.

Quit stalling.

Okay, you can put on one dot of perfume first. The patchouli-based scent the makeup artist had tucked into her bag was heavy and musky, generating images of long, steamy afternoons of sex, which meant she had to keep Carter interested until summertime.

Maybe she was starting too soon.

Get yourself across the hall!

She sneaked across the sitting room floor, positioned herself outside Carter's door—

She'd forgotten the sheaf of papers she was supposed to wave in his face.

Back across the sitting room. Grab the papers. Back to Carter's door. No nonsense now. Go for it.

She threw open his door with a shattering bang. "Carter, I've had a brainstorm!" she announced, scurrying into the room before he could find something to throw at her. "Wake up. I have to talk to you now, while it's fresh on my mind." She'd reached his bed, where he was thrashing, trying to sit up. She plopped herself onto the edge and drew one knee up until it touched him.

"Is it morning?" he croaked.

"Not yet. This is too important to wait for morning." The act of parting her legs like that, feeling the robe slide open and the cool air of the room wafting between her thighs, all that while being so close to Carter's overwhelming maleness was having a startling effect on her. It was Carter she was supposed to be seducing, not herself.

She put the sheaf of papers on the other side of him, which gave her all the excuse she needed to lean over him, brushing his chest with her breasts. He seemed to be trying to pull more cover over himself, but her position made it impossible. "Can you wake up enough to listen?"

HE WAS AS AWAKE AS he'd ever been in his entire life. His eyes might not be fully open, but under the covers, everything was stirring. In the light that came through the doorway he could see her clearly enough to react to the silkiness of the robe she was wearing, and how little there was of it. Her knee pushed against his thigh and the robe parted, giving him a glimpse of her breasts, smooth, creamy, mounded like ice cream and just begging to be licked. The robe was pink. Strawberry sauce.

She wore a gown under the robe, but it concealed

nothing. His hands were itching to slide into that opening in the robe, cup her breasts, bring them to his mouth one at a time, discover and explore her nipples. He wanted to make her scream with pleasure and beg him for more.

His erection, sudden and powerful, ached insistently.

"There's a thread that runs through all the depositions," she said, but his senses went on the alert when she moved a little closer, bent a little lower, then put her hand on his chest, splaying out the fingers. It was such a small gesture, and undoubtedly an innocent one. She had no idea how her touch branded him with its heat. He mustn't let himself reach out to her. If he touched her, he would have to kiss her, wouldn't be able to help himself.

Just like he couldn't help shifting under the pressure of her smooth, slim hand, turning the touch into a stroke, feeling her fingernails rasp lightly against his chest hair, making it tickle, making his own nipples harden with pleasure and anticipation.

The scent of her perfume wafted to his nose, not overpowering but intriguing, something rich, mysterious and suggestive. The gleam of her hair, the flash of her eyes, were casting a spell on him.

She felt it, too. He could tell by the way her voice slowed, thickened until it sounded like dark honey. "They all want something," she said, but her eyes had fixed on his face, and those long lashes were drooping down to her cheeks.

Did it mean there was a limit to her self-control? But was she feeling anything important for him, or was it just her excitement at having made a discovery? Or, just as hopeless, was it just a natural but impersonal reaction to the intimacy of being alone in a dark bedroom with someone, nearly naked? And did he even care?

God, how he wanted to pull her down to him and take her mouth so hard and fast that she'd want him to take the rest of her just as hard and fast. "Everybody wants something," he managed to say, hearing how his voice has hoarsened. He was desperate to tell her what he wanted. No, to show her, with his mouth, his tongue, his hands, his cock that throbbed so painfully with longing to be inside her.

That was more than he could hope for, no matter what happened.

"Yes," she said, starting to sound a little uneven, "and the interesting thing about these witnesses is that they all want the same thing. They want...they want..."

His heart stood still as her mouth came closer and closer, and suddenly she was there, her lips against his, his arms around her, his hands roaming that long, slim, sweet body. Then, at last, with a moan that vibrated through him, she straightened out her endless, silky legs and he tugged her on top of him, stretching her out over the full length of his body.

She was already in a state of such ecstasy she didn't know how she could bear anymore. He was all male hardness, the tongue that tangled with hers, the hands that gripped her buttocks and molded her against the hardest, most demanding part of him. In an agony of suspended desire she parted her thighs and their bodies meshed, all heat and wetness, and she instinctively moved against him, relishing the power of him as she sought the release she needed so desperately.

He kissed her with a passion that needed no words, no explaining. His chest pressed against her breasts.

Her nipples ached with pleasure, and she moved against him there, too, feeling the crisp hair against her skin, maddened by it, dissolving in a pool of liquid fire.

"We can't do this." He tried to push her away, but she knew his heart wasn't in it, nor was the rest of his body.

"Yes, we can," she said, breathing the words into his ear. She felt quite determined about it. "We *are* doing it."

"No, no, we shouldn't...oh, God," he said as she darted her tongue between his lips and seized his mouth again.

She nibbled her way along his jaw. "Why shouldn't we?"

"You don't really want to is why," he panted as her lips reached his neck. "It's just the moment. It's the night and the Christmas season and the tension of the case..."

With a soft oof, she found herself stretched out beside him. It was nice, but not where she wanted to be. "What's wrong with any of that?" she asked, her voice so husky with need, she could barely speak.

"Oh, Mallory," he said. "Nothing, except—you're going to respect me even less in the morning." Before she could organize her mind enough to ask what he meant by that, his arm went swiftly around her and his mouth came down to hers.

They'd passed the point of no return.

10

SHE WAS MORE THAN he'd imagined she'd be, sweeter, softer, hotter, a crème brûlée straight from the broiler, all cream and sugary crunch. She protested with a delicious little squeak when he broke off the kiss that was carrying them too far too fast, but when he took the small shell of her ear between his teeth and nibbled at it, he heard her breath quicken.

He wanted to take his time with her. It wouldn't be easy—his mind was telling him slow and careful while his body craved hard and fast. But if he was going to be nothing more to her than a toy, something to relieve the sexual need she was surprising him with, then he was going to be the best sex toy she would ever possess.

And possess him she had. He didn't know when or how. The one thing he did know was that he wanted nothing but her, wanted to touch every part of her. He loved leaning over her like this, pinning down a willing wanton who shivered when his tongue explored the inside of her ear. Then she moaned as he trailed kisses down her cheek, finally burying his face in her neck, nipping and kissing as his hand went of its own accord to one of those mounded breasts he hadn't been able to get off his mind.

She arched against him, burying her face in his shoulder, and the breast filled his hand, so firm, the skin so velvety, the nipple a small, hard knot. A surge of animal desire rocked him, and he pulled himself back. He couldn't imagine she was very experienced in lovemaking, but even if she was, even if there were a secret Mallory he'd never dreamt of, he wanted to give her the most, be the best.

Caressing her breast, he was filled with the need to see the nipple that pressed against his palm, to circle it with his thumb, lick it, fill his mouth with it. His hand went to the shoulder of her robe and tugged it away. His heart leaped when he saw she was helping him, shrugging out of the robe, attempting to slither out of the gown.

"I have an extrication plan." He heard the harshness of desire in his voice, hoped she recognized it for what it was, the voice of a man who was attempting intelligent speech when he was well beyond it. He trailed his fingers down the center front of the gown, found its hem and began to gather it up in his fingertips, sliding his knuckles between her thighs and pausing to nest in the soft, silky mound of hair he encountered next. She moaned, bent her knees, thrust against his hand.

"Mmm," he murmured, "I can't wait until morning."

"Why?" she gasped.

"To see if your hair is the same color all over."

"Want...to make...a bet now?" The words were challenging, but not her voice. Everything else about her felt yielding, meltingly soft.

"Yeah." He pressed a little harder with his knuckles, reveling in the way she wriggled against him. "I'll bet you breakfast in bed that it's not."

"I'll, umm, bet you breakfast in bed it...is—oh, my God, what are you doing, what..."

His knuckles had found their mark, the tiny, secret nub he would seek again and again, with his knuckles, his fingertips, his tongue and his throbbing penis before the night was over. She parted her legs, arching her body as if she were craving his touch. He heard another little cry of protest when he moved on, gathering up the gown, pausing for only a second between her breasts, and that was for his own pleasure, to revisit that valley of firm creaminess.

At last the gown was over her head and tossed into a corner. He gathered that long, slim, silky body into both his arms, stroking down her back to mold her to him, felt her wetness soothing his painful hardness and thought he wouldn't care if he died right now. Nothing could feel better than this, except the sensation of her hands raking his skin from shoulder blades to buttocks, driving him to frenzy and making him fight for control of his male animal body, which wanted only release from the pressure of the tide rising inside him.

He sank his mouth to her breasts to wait out the wave. Her nipples were small and hard. That would be another thing he'd know in the morning, if they were pink as he imagined them to be, the pink of her lips. The only thing he was certain of now was that they were delicious. With her velvet breast cupped in his hand and her nipple in his mouth, he reveled in the heat of her writhing body. He would torture it, torment it, until she begged him to finish what he'd begun.

He'd finish, in time, but there was so much more he wanted to explore, touch, stroke. He moved away from her breasts, scattering kisses down her bare flesh to her navel, to what he now knew would be the same silvery-blond of her hair. He sank his face into it, breathing in her woman's scent, powerful and erotic, before his tongue at last found that tiny hidden nub and laved it, devoured it.

She was liquid beneath his touch, lava that flowed, slow and hot, and that same lava seemed to flow through his own veins. But he could feel the moment when she could think only of her own desire and he eased his fingers inside her where she was wet and slick with desire, massaging the swollen little knot outside with his thumb.

She screamed when she came, explosively, her head flung back, the quintessential woman in the throes of pleasure.

Mallory, screaming. It was a concept he couldn't get his mind around, but it didn't matter, because he'd stopped thinking with his mind a long time ago and the only concept he could handle was getting that hard, throbbing part of him inside her and staying there until he screamed, too.

Just not yet. Hugging her close to him, he groaned.

SO THIS IS BLISS. Collapsed in his arms, still zinging from the spasms that had rocked her minutes before, she wanted to pinch herself to make sure it wasn't just a dream born of her deepest desires. Nothing like this had ever happened to her. A few brief, unsatisfying affairs that ended by mutual agreement and with equal relief, but not a moment of them had felt like this. She'd vowed to feel this with Carter and at last, at long last, it was happening. She must have been holding out for him all these years.

She snuggled a little deeper into his shoulder, touched her mouth to his throat, felt him stir beside her. He'd been nibbling her earlobe, and now his mouth slid to her cheek, strung kisses down to her chin. She tried capturing it on its way, but he had an agenda of his own and she'd just have to wait until he'd kissed her breasts, tickled the nipples with his tongue while the hair on his chest tickled even more sensitive parts of her. She moved against him, surprised to feel the aching heat rise inside her again. There was something else she wanted, something she'd daydreamed about. Surely he wouldn't mind.

Her sweat-slick body slid over his until she was straddling him, until she could feel that delicious hardness pressing into the most sensitive part of her. With a low sound of surprise he adjusted himself beneath her, cupped her buttocks in his hands and raked them gently, dipping lower with each stroke in a way that would surely drive her mad if she didn't move, hard and fast. She began to rock against him, the ache building higher and stronger. He bucked beneath her, matching her rhythm, urging her on, and when the spasms consumed her again she cried out, "Inside me. I want you inside me now," knowing it was the one more thing she had to have to feel complete.

"Shh," he whispered back. "In a minute, in a minute..."

"Oh, oh..." The shudders were traveling through her like earthquake tremors, shattering her with their power. "Now, please, now," she moaned, and somehow he was protected and there where she wanted him to be, above her, taking control, slipping inside her. She gasped at the heat and hardness of him and he took her gently at first. Then overcome by his own need he was driving, thrusting, pounding into her as she arched to meet him, feeling his desperate urgency and begging him to share her pleasure, until at last, with a shout, he drove into her one last time and they collapsed together into the deep, aching quivers of release.

Hot and wet, he clung to her, easing to her side but not letting go, not letting her feel alone, and she lay there in his arms, panting in the cool air of night.

"Are you sorry?" Her voice came in a faint, exhausted whisper.

"No." He took her earlobe in his teeth and nibbled it gently. "Are you?"

"Uh-uh. It was nice."

"Nice. Nice?" She felt his smile against her cheek.

"Extremely nice."

"I'm sure I can do better than that." His hands began a slow, tantalizing exploration of her entire body. The night was only beginning.

If this was all she could have of him, she would still treasure this one night. She'd made it happen, taken it for herself in an act of boldness she hadn't dreamed she was capable of, and she would hold it forever in her heart, even if she couldn't have Carter forever in her arms.

"WOW, WE PRETTY MUCH destroyed everything." Carter sat up in bed and viewed the chaos of her bedroom with apparent satisfaction.

Still half asleep and lying on her stomach, Mallory trailed her hand along the carpeting and came up with several pieces of foil which she tossed carelessly toward the wastepaper basket. Some of them actually landed inside. "I do admire your presence of mind," she said before she yawned, "in remembering the condoms when we decided to change bedrooms."

"You're not the only one who's prepared."

"I'm not giving up the gold medal," Mallory said,

"but I will raise your handicap a little." She was still wearing her watch, and she glanced at it, surprised it had survived the night's acrobatics. "Good thing it's Saturday."

"Yep. We'd be in big trouble if it weren't."

She might be in big trouble now. She felt his arms sliding under hers, felt herself being turned over. "Moment of truth," he said, his eyes skimming down her naked body.

For a second she was afraid he was going to say he knew how deliberate her raid on him the night before had been, until she saw where his gaze had settled. "Ha," she said, amazed at how unself-conscious she felt, "you lose."

He ran his fingers through her pubic hair, which was, in fact, pale blond, making her shift restlessly against the sheets. "I wouldn't call it *losing*," he said, then sighed regretfully. "I'm not sure I can go on until I've had coffee and a shower."

"That's okay," Mallory said, "though it wasn't what I'd hoped for from you, but I... Carter, don't you dare. Stop it right now. I was only kidding. We need coffee. Showers. Breakfast. I want to brush my teeth... Carter..."

"BREAKFAST IN BED is definitely called for," Carter announced quite a while later.

"It's the only way we're going to get any," Mallory agreed.

"I'll call room service. You think of something we can do while we wait." He waggled his eyebrows at her.

"Make the call. I'll come up with a plan."

He couldn't wait to see what the plan was. Five

minutes later, after he'd ordered a breakfast appropriate for farmworkers during haying season, he shouted her name.

"In here," she called back.

"In where?" But he knew where. Her bathroom door was open, and no one could miss the cloud of steam rising above the shower. His groin tightened as he played her hide-and-seek game, and when he drew close to the shower door, it opened swiftly and she reached out and grabbed him, tugging him inside with her.

"Just think of the water we're saving," he murmured, tantalizing himself by holding her away from him for a moment. She was exquisite naked, with her hair slicked down and her eyelashes sparkling with water droplets. Her pale skin was pink from the heat and irresistible to the touch, and her nipples, softer now from the warmth, were also pink, just as he'd imagined. They needed touching, it was obvious.

He reached out for the soap, massaged it between his hands into a thick lather and covered her breasts with it. She shivered and closed her eyes. "That's right. Let me make you clean all over." The only thing between his palms and her skin were the slick bubbles, and under his caress he felt those beautiful, small pink nipples harden in spite of the heat.

His arousal increased as he slid the lather over her stomach, her back, her arms, her legs, her buttocks. She slipped and slid against him, moving against his skin in the most maddening, provocative way. He began to slide down, down, until he'd reached the wettest golden hair and put his mouth against the warm crevice in which he'd taken such pleasure in the night.

She moaned, tangling her fingers in his hair, leaning

on him for support and pressing him tighter into that crevice all at the same time. He was in heaven, not even minding the increasing urgency in his own body, and was distraught to feel her suddenly grow still.

"What?" His voice was hoarse.

"It's the doorbell."

"Ignore it." He resumed his exploration with his tongue.

"It's the waiter. We have to—"

"Don't have to do anything." He was undistractable. "He'll let himself in, leave breakfast—"

She was pushing him away, but she was laughing, a delicious, throaty laugh. "I'm not that sophisticated. Let him in and keep him out of here."

With great reluctance he got up off his knees, then almost returned there at the sight of her heavy-lidded eyes, the pout of her desire-swollen mouth. "Go," she whispered.

He put on the hotel robe without drying himself off and pulled her tight against him. "So much I didn't know about you," he murmured.

"Like what?"

"Didn't know you ever kidded anybody, for one thing. Didn't know you could make love and laugh at the same time. Didn't know..."

Didn't know you could want me so much, or make me feel this way.

The depth of the emotion he felt scared him. "Didn't know you could wait this long for your morning coffee," he said, gave her bottom a little spank, and went to receive breakfast.

In a very short time they were propped up in bed devouring eggs and bacon, English muffins and sweet rolls, juice and coffee. "Um-yum," Mallory said, slathering ginger marmalade on a piece of muffin.

When he figured she'd had enough food to subsist on for a while, he let his arm drop casually around her shoulders, then tightened it and pressed her against his stubborn erection.

"You can't possibly want more," she moaned.

"Why stop now?" he said reasonably, because he did want more, as soon as possible, "The damage is done. We came to New York to work together and found out it was fun to play together, too."

"I guess you could look at it that way." She moved a little closer to him, but he sensed something different in her and wondered if he'd said the wrong thing.

Not knowing what he might have said wrong, he went on in the same cheerful vein. "That's the fine line between a solicitor, which you are, and a barrister, which I am, if I may use the English system as an example," he lectured. "We barristers can rationalize anything."

"Do we have to rationalize this?" True, her face was buried in his shoulder, but her voice sounded so faint that he was increasingly sure he'd hurt her in some way. Not knowing what to do about it, he tried tenderness.

"Again, that's what makes a solicitor," he said, dropping little kisses on the parts of her he could reach. "Always with the questions, always after the facts."

Yes, he did need to rationalize this, but he didn't want to explain that he was too awed by her organized, retentive mind to feel worthy of her. So what? It was fun just being her boy toy. He kissed her a little more purposefully, feeling her respond, wondering if sex was the only way he could reach her.

"Don't tip over the tray," she said, already sounding breathless. "We'll get butter and crumbs all over us."

"Breaded for frying," he agreed, ignoring the precarious tray and blowing the words onto her neck, that spot just below her ear that seemed to turn her on.

She shivered. "Buttered for eating," she said, and then, "Forget I said that."

"I can't," he said regretfully. "It's given me ideas. Not butter exactly, but...how about marmalade?" He grabbed the spoon, dunked it in the marmalade dish and plopped the spoonful directly onto that enchanting puff of golden hair.

"Carter! I just showered! Now look at me! I'm all sticky!"

"Yum," Carter growled, embarking on the delightful task of licking her clean.

He'd apparently restored her good mood. He had just one more problem to deal with. He had no desire to do anything today but stay in bed with Mallory, but he had to sneak away somehow for his third appointment with Maybelle Ewing. The woman was crazy, definitely. Anybody with seventeen diplomas on the wall had to be crazy, but what she'd been saying to him made sense.

He wasn't a bad kid anymore, hadn't been for years, and it was possible nobody thought of him that way except himself. It wasn't his image he needed to change, Maybelle had declared after talking to him about three minutes yesterday, it was his attitude.

She'd also told him that what he had to deal with was easy compared with the changes another client of hers was having to make. "That girl," Maybelle said, "don't know she's a doll, don't know she's sexy as all get-out, don't unnerstand that anybody in the world'd give his right...arm to have her. You think you aren't smart. She thinks smart's *all* she is. Like I said, you've got it easy."

He was sure he could think up an excuse to get away for that three o'clock appointment. After a little more caffeine and a little more love-in-the-morning.

HER APPOINTMENT WITH Maybelle was at four that afternoon, and Maybelle had announced they'd be having tea at Lady Mendl's Tea Salon in New York's Gramercy Park. Mallory had thought several times of telling Maybelle that she wasn't *that* put off by the horned desk, and now that they'd outfitted her they could resume the meetings in Maybelle's office, but Maybelle hadn't given her a chance. Tea on a wintry afternoon sounded wonderful, anyway. She hoped Lady Mendl's offered an extensive tea with scones and sandwiches, éclairs and butter cookies. She had to come up with a plausible reason to separate her body from Carter's, and she'd finally hit upon one.

"I have an appointment to have my hair trimmed this afternoon," she told him over the clam chowder and crabcakes they had for lunch at the little round table in the sitting room. "I may be gone a couple of hours. I need a few things, panty hose..." She trailed off. Was it her imagination, or had a look of relief crossed Carter's face? She could hardly blame him. She was exhausted. And ravenous. She rarely ate more than a salad for lunch, and she was attacking these crabcakes as if she hadn't eaten in days.

Carter had asked for two orders for himself and had offered her the same option. "They're small," he'd explained. "That would be a good idea for me, too," he said. "I could use a haircut, and I'm out of shaving cream."

"I couldn't tell." She sent him a secret smile.

"You'd be able to by tomorrow."

So he wasn't bored yet. That was good news. "Okay, then, we can take off at—"

"I'd like to leave at about two-thirty," he interrupted her. "I might catch the end of the football game if I get an early start."

"I'll hang around a little while longer and get my clothes in order for next week. I should be home by five-thirty."

She eyed him, noticing that he seemed to be eyeing her in the same way, the way people look at each other when they haven't told the whole truth.

Her lie, of course, was perfectly innocent. She'd pick up some panty hose at Saks and dart into one of those no-appointment places that were all over New York for a trim, all before tea. She just wasn't mentioning her appointment with Maybelle, that was all. Carter's plan, she had a feeling, wasn't quite so innocent.

Maybe he had to tell somebody goodbye. Forever.

Maybe he had to keep somebody on the string until he got bored with Mallory.

Maybe he needed a haircut and shaving cream, but his hair looked fine to her. And everywhere his face had touched her, it had felt wonderfully smooth. She shivered.

"WHAT I THINK, JACK," Maybelle said to Carter, "is that you've fallen for somebody and you're afraid you're not good enough for her."

"I don't know—*fallen* might be going too far. Or maybe not. I sure have been obsessing about her. As for good enough, well, maybe I'm *good* enough, just not *smart* enough. Or maybe I'm even smart enough. I just can't get anybody to see me that way." He felt dazed from too much breakfast, too much lunch, too much arousal, not enough sleep and not enough information about where the hell Mallory had to go this afternoon. There'd been something evasive in the way she'd mentioned her haircut. He knew enough about women to know haircuts didn't take two hours.

Of course, he hadn't been telling the truth, either, but he knew what he was lying about and it was perfectly innocent.

"Way-ell, tell me about your girl," Maybelle said. "How y'all met. Mebbe somethin'll click in my mind."

"I've known her a long time. We were in law school together."

"Y'all are both lawyers?"

"Yeah."

"That's a coincidence," Maybelle said, more to herself than to him.

"Not really," Carter said. "People do meet in law school. We did. We studied together."

"Studied together? Nuthin' else?"

"Nope."

"You didn't think she was pretty?"

"Yes, I thought she was pretty."

"Just not sexy."

"She didn't act very, um, accessible," Carter admitted.

"Okay, so y'all have known each other awhile without doin' nuthin' about it and suddenly you want to do something about it. What changed?"

"She did," Carter blurted out. "I mean, she didn't really. Just sort of."

"What'd she change? Her hair? Her clothes?"

"Not her hair," he said very fast. "She'd better not ever change her hair. Her hair..." He was getting aroused thinking about her damned *hair*. "It's like corn silk, but even lighter colored than corn silk...and not as slimy," he finished up.

Maybelle's expression changed. It was an infinitesimal change, but Carter had spent too much time in the courtroom not to notice the nuances in people's faces. He gazed at her closely.

"Anybody ever tell y'all you had the soul of a poet?" was what she said.

"No."

"They was right not to. So she didn't change her hair. What about her clothes?"

"She always looked nice," Carter said, turning his pen between his fingers. "It was just that her clothes didn't make you think there was a body under them."

"And they do now?"

Carter frowned. "Well, after I ruined her black suit..."

Maybelle jolted visibly in her chair.

"You okay?" he said.

"Jes' a twinge of arthuritis, hon. Go on. How'd y'all ruin the suit?"

"I sprayed mustard on it. Then she showed up in this red jacket..." He paused because Maybelle had flipped her ubiquitous coffee cup straight up in the air.

"Oh, shoot," she said, but she sounded really nervous. "Dickie!" she shrieked. "Come here and bring me some a them paper towels."

Yep, she was crazy. Here he was, facing the most important passage of his life, and he'd put himself in the hands of a certified nutcase.

That's how smart he was. Pick up a card in a hotel hallway and sure! Dial the number! If Mallory knew, he could kiss goodbye to any notion of gaining her respect.

11

MAYBELLE WAS NEVER LATE, so Mallory had a right to notice when, this time, she was. She whooshed in like a blue norther, wearing a coat that had once been a patchwork quilt, the kind made of different-size patches in a multitude of colors.

"Sorry, hon," she said as she ignored the coat-check woman and instead used the back of her chair to hold the coat, where its arms flopped down to the floor like lobster claws. "Have I ever had me a day." Under the coat she was dressed in her usual good taste—jeans, of course, with a top that seemed to be made of tiny skins stitched together.

Dozens of defenseless mice had died in the making of that top, Mallory decided. Or perhaps newts left over from witches' spells.

Maybelle saw her looking at it. "It's that fake suede stuff," she said. "I designed it myself. I like an animal theme to my clothes. Kindly iss-stablishes a bond with 'em, y'know?"

"It's lovely," Mallory said politely. "I'm sorry you had a bad day. Are you having a problem, or is it one of your clients?"

She was surprised to see Maybelle tighten her lips. "I'm not sayin' another word about any of my clients. Dickie's always tellin' me I'm too loose-lipped. I thought if I didn't mention names—I mean, I don't mean nobody no harm, I just think they're all so intrestin'. But not anymore. I'm straight-nin' up and flyin' straight." She frowned deeply to indicate how serious she was, and her face collapsed into a million fine wrinkles.

"I sense that something happened to make you feel this way," Mallory said.

"It didn't happen yet," Maybelle said darkly, "but it might. Now, hon, your turn. Did y'all's plan work last night?"

Mallory nodded. "We had a breakthrough," was all she said, since she didn't intend to discuss her sex life with anybody. For one thing, she so rarely had a sex life to discuss that she hadn't gotten in the habit.

"Way-ell, good." Maybelle peered at her. "Y'all think it was all them clothes and shoes, all that makeup?"

"What else could it have been?" Mallory asked, puzzled by the question.

"It coulda been just you," Maybelle said wistfully, "finally havin' a chance ta catch the man you always wanted."

Mallory drew in a sharp breath. Maybelle was too close to the truth.

"And the way you did it was you finally *veered*."

"You've been reading my mother's book."

"Ever' word of it."

"What did you think?"

Maybelle sighed. "You was right, hon. Me readin' it saved us a world of time. Yore mamma and yore daddy made you the way you are, a real sweet thing, but y'all got your priorities all mixed up."

Now Mallory really felt stunned. "My priorities are not all mixed up," she protested. "An orderly life has to come first. It's the only way to keep your head straight."

"And your heart under lock and key waitin' for you to get finished cleanin' up yore house," Maybelle said, a bit too loudly for Mallory's comfort. She dived into a handbag that was a kangaroo with a zipper across the front, whipped out Ellen Trent's book and slammed it on the table. Everyone in the small, elegant tearoom looked up. "This is a real good book," Maybelle said, "but it's not a real good life for anybody but yore sainted mother, pardon my French."

"Would you ladies like tea, or did you come here merely to break up the furniture?" A haughty waiter stared down at them with the purest disgust.

As Maybelle sent a similar look back up at him, her eyes widened. "Dee-wayne, is that you?"

The man took another look at her and his face lit up. "Maybelle, as I live and breathe. Yes, indeed, it is I. And how are you, dear lady?"

"Doin' real good," Maybelle said, then added with a brief glower, "most days, anyways." Her face cleared, became all sunshine again. "And look at y'all!" she said conspiratorially. "All spiffied up and workin' in this ritzy place."

"Thanks to you." He practically genuflected. "Incidentally, Maybelle, it's been a year now and you still haven't sent me a bill. I was wondering..."

Maybelle did that diamond-crusted wave of the hand that was her signature mannerism. "Yeah, I gotta get around to that one of these days. But we can't tawk bidness now. We're ready for tea. Bring us everything, and heavy on that there Devonshire cream."

MALLORY HELD UP A hand to signal a cab to take her back to the St. Regis. Maybelle had a way of leaving her with sound bites instead of actual advice. And the sound bite sticking with her now was "This is a real good book, but it's not a real good life for anybody but yore sainted mother."

Hadn't the last week told her that? That the happiest moment of her life was waking up in chaos with Carter this morning? That the best Christmas tree she'd ever had was the tiny tree in the suite that was even now dropping needles all over the table? That the best man she'd ever known was Carter Compton, who waited there for her now with his possessions scattered over every flat surface? And that she'd had to give up a lot of herself to get to this point in her life? She hadn't merely veered, she'd spun and twisted and thrashed and...

"Taxi!" Waving wildly, she shouted the word so vehemently that a cab half a block away, a cab which, furthermore, had an Off Duty sign flashing on its roof, changed its trajectory and screeched to a halt with the door handle directly ahead of her outstretched hand.

SHE FOUND CARTER hunched in front of the sitting room television set, his shoulders moving along with the Northwestern quarterback's, shouting words of encouragement to his favorite team. He was wearing black jeans with a black turtleneck and looked absolutely heavenly. The jeans hugged his thighs and the heavy muscles there flexed as his shoulders moved, his biceps rose and fell, his teeth clenched and relaxed. Scattered around him were the sofa pillows, a newspaper, a soft drink can, an open bag of microwave popcorn, the remote control, his shoes, his overshoes, his scarf, gloves, overcoat—

There was some hope for him. He'd apparently brought just one coat with him to New York. She smiled.

"Hey," he said when he caught sight of her. "We're only behind fourteen points. It's a moral victory!"

Football hadn't been on her family's weekend schedule. Her father preferred war movies. Her mother wouldn't attend or watch anything she didn't consider to be culturally uplifting and therefore worth an efficient woman's time. Macon played football on the computer occasionally. Stepping toward Carter, intending to join him, perhaps attack and distract him, even learn about football if that was what it took, she saw that the tiny Christmas tree was circled with a string of old-fashioned bubble lights. Her heart pounded with something that went deeper than desire—honest affection.

She slid onto the sofa beside him, dropping her Saks bag to the floor. "Come on, baby, light my tree," she sang.

"Just a minute, just a minute... Defense!" he shouted, nearly sending her sailing off the cushion. "Sorry," he said immediately. "What did you say?"

"It can wait," she said, snuggling back in beside him and wishing she knew how to purr.

He'd had a haircut. He'd bought shaving cream and lights for their Christmas tree. She was in love.

THEY CELEBRATED Northwestern's moral victory with a bottle of champagne. They made love on the sofa, sitting up, Mallory straddling him, enveloping him, her body and her heart zinging with lust and love and an overwhelming desire to be with him forever.

Her clothes, she observed later, were scattered from

the kitchen, where the lovemaking had begun, to the front door, where Carter's football-throwing arm had propelled her new red lace bra. The new black suit from Bergdorf's was mainly wool with a smidgen of Lycra and the wrinkles steamed out beautifully while they lay together in a bubble bath.

Mallory felt it was pure good luck that her bathroom was equipped with a bathtub and a separate shower, European-style. Carter had resisted the notion of bathing in the tub, insisting that real men didn't take bubble baths, that he'd never had a bubble bath and wasn't about to start now, but once she was ensconced in the tub, hidden by bubbles except for her toes, which she wriggled enticingly at him, he changed his mind. They could call it *her* bubble bath, he said. He was just visiting.

He rinsed her hair with the leftover champagne. The bath led them inevitably back to bed. Dinner was paté, cheese, crusty Italian bread, fruit and Napoleons from room service. While they ate, they watched the Christmas episode of Carter's favorite network series, a police drama.

It was a heartwarming story about a passerby finding a young couple and their new baby huddled in a Dumpster under a streetlamp near the police station. Three top-ranked mounted police rode their horses to the scene, bearing an envelope filled with cash contributed by the guys at the station, a basket of baby powders, oils and diapers and a gift certificate for a week's stay in a motel in New Jersey. The plot was a timeworn one, but the emotional level was high and Mallory couldn't help shedding a tear or two.

They were cuddled together on the sofa, Mallory in a

short black nightgown, Carter in preppy plaid boxers, when he said, "As you were saying..."

She raised her head from his shoulder. "When?"

He held her a little tighter. "Last night when you bopped into my room. You said you'd had an idea that might work with Phoebe and her plaintiffs."

She sighed, sinking down on his chest. "I can't imagine I ever had an idea. Oh, wait, it's coming back."

It had been a crazy, pop-psychology idea she'd dreamed up as an excuse to seduce Carter in her new pink gown and robe, but she could hardly tell him that. "I was just thinking that everybody wants something really badly. Like, for example, we know from his testimony that Kevin Knightson wants to break into show business, and McGregor Ross wants her daughter to be a child model."

"She ought to be prepping the kid for college," Carter said.

"I know," Mallory said, "but she doesn't want what you and I would want." She paused, feeling somewhat embarrassed. "I mean what you would want or I would want."

"I get your point."

"Once upon a time," Mallory went on, relieved that he hadn't read anything possessive into her words, "the plaintiffs seemed satisfied to have themselves and their bathrooms back to normal. Phoebe convinced them they wanted more."

"Money."

"Yes, and everybody wants money, but I'm suggesting we try to find out what they want more than money."

"Hmm," Carter said.

Mallory persisted. "There's probably something you want more than money, right?"

RIGHT. I WANT TO settle this case just to hear you tell me I'm a brilliant lawyer.

And that you'd like nothing more than to add a brilliant lawyer to your life, maybe even have a brilliant kid or two.

Okay, I know I'm not brilliant, but I am smarter than people imagine, and I really hope I never get another call like that call from Bill Decker, because I want to lose the Casanova image and settle down with...

A jolt of electricity ran through Carter's body, but it was more like a security alarm than the electricity Mallory generated in him. These were serious thoughts. Maybe too serious for a man who'd seen a woman change from good old Mallory to the object of his desire in the course of an extremely tense week.

"It's not a bad idea," Mallory was saying, "but I don't have the faintest idea how to implement it. We can't get Kevin a role on Broadway. I don't know any Broadway producers or directors. Do you?" She yawned.

He smiled into her hair. Even without the yawn he would have known she was getting sleepy. She wasn't usually such a chatterbox. "We take it one step at a time," he said. "First we find out what they want."

"How?"

"Ask them."

"What a great idea." Her eyes drooped, and then she said, "Our tree needs more ornaments."

"We'll buy some tomorrow."

"I'll buy some. You bought the lights."

"You don't think we can charge it all to our expense accounts?"

"No."

"I was afraid you'd feel that way," Carter said.

"And so do you."

She was right. He'd never cheat on an expense account. But how did she know that?

"WE SHOULD CALL Bill before we leave this morning," Mallory said on Monday. She was wearing one of those longish skirts with the jacket that matched her eyes, and Carter got hot all over remembering the sheer tank she'd worn underneath the week before. Tonight when they got home, he'd get her out of the jacket fast, explore her through that tank top. He growled.

"What?"

"Ah. Right. Call Bill. We can run your idea by him, see if he thinks we can do something with it."

But a half hour later, Mallory said, "He didn't sound particularly enthusiastic, did he?"

"He doesn't have your imagination. I'm still adding that question to my spiel—'What do you really want?' We can see if a pattern emerges, something we can work with."

What he couldn't tell Mallory was that Bill had his own idea about settling the case, that Carter take Phoebe up on one of her none-too-subtle suggestions that they have dinner, catch a show, watch a television special. At her place.

That second week of depositions, she intensified her pursuit. All Mallory had to do was take a break to powder her nose between sessions with the witnesses and Phoebe was on his case in a flash.

"Just because we're professional opponents," she usually ended up saying, "doesn't mean we can't be personal friends."

He pled busyness, prior engagements, tiredness, which was the truth. Because he lived for the nights, when he and Mallory could drop their cool daytime exteriors and give in to the consuming heat of their lovemaking.

Friday night, after another long week of deposing witnesses, Mallory produced a copy of the court reporter's transcript and suggested they start weeding through it for clues to the special desires of the witnesses.

Carter had other ideas as to how they might spend their time, which he freely shared with her.

"We can work in bed," she said, fluttering her eyelashes at him.

"Oh, okay," he said, giving in.

He brushed his teeth, did a touch-up shave and went to her room, where she'd begun setting things up for the job they were going to do. He found her wearing a Santa Claus hat. Just a Santa Claus hat, he was pretty sure, although she'd drawn the covers up modestly beneath her chin.

"Ho, ho, ho," he said, and climbed into the other side. He'd hoped his flipping up the covers would answer his question about what she was or was not wearing, but was foiled by the computer on her lap and the stacks of papers that surrounded her.

"I thought we'd get into the spirit," she said, and smashed an identical hat down on his head. "I'm calling this the All-I-Want-for-Christmas project."

"I feel like an idiot," Carter muttered.

"You look like one, too," Mallory said, "but those of us on the inside track know you're not." She turned to face him directly, and she smiled. "You are masterful at interrogating those witnesses. You're pleasant and polite, but you don't give an inch. And you always seem to have the right question at your fingertips. I am so impressed. It's a special talent."

The words sang in his ears. This was what he'd wanted most to hear from her. It made everything all right where Mallory was concerned. He still had to convince Bill, but Mallory's opinion was the only one that really mattered. His heart zinging with joy, he scaled the stack of printout and the laptop and gave her a thorough kiss.

"There, we got that out of the way," he said after he was able to talk himself into letting her go. "Now I can return to my favorite activity, which is working on Friday night. Straighten your hat," he ordered her. "It looks too sexy tilted like that."

"Yes, dear." She tugged the hat down over her hair. He loved the breathless sound of her voice.

But she buckled right down to work. Methodically they read through the transcript and highlighted the responses from the witnesses that might indicate their deepest wishes. On the laptop, Mallory listed the witness's name, the page on which the response appeared and a brief summary of the response.

"Do you have to be so organized?" he complained.

"Yes," she said.

"Okay." He shrugged. Whatever it took to make her happy, he felt he could handle it. He went back to work with his green highlighter.

An hour later, they'd already assembled this much information:

Kevin Knightson: *One good part in a production, stage or screen.*

Tammy Sue Teezer: *I want to be in a commercial and*

make tons of money and buy a house in the country and a great big dog.

McGregor Ross: *I want everybody in the world to know I have the most beautiful baby ever born.*

Trent: *I'm sure she is.*

Compton: *I'm sure she is.*

McGregor Ross: *And I want her to win the Wiggles Diapers Poster Baby contest.*

Compton: (Inaudible)

Trent: (Inaudible)

"You didn't have to type the whole conversation," Carter said, complaining again, because he really felt like moving on to Phases Two, Three, Four and perhaps Five of the evening.

"It was too funny not to," Mallory said, pursing her pretty pink lips.

They worked awhile longer. "There's a strong show-biz theme here, Carter," she observed.

"And it's a pretty logical assumption," Carter said. "People who dye their hair this carroty-red color, or try to," he added with a wince, "are making a statement."

"Trying to get noticed," Mallory agreed.

"Doing something so different that it catches the eye."

Mallory sighed. "Sounds like we're going to have to put on a show in daddy's barn."

"What are you talking about?"

She turned to him. "Didn't you ever watch those old black-and-white movies with Judy Garland and Mickey Rooney?"

"You mean the ones about putting on a show?"

"Uh-huh."

"Judy and Mickey were going to put on a show to raise money for the school or the band or a field trip?"

"Yes, those."

"No, I never watched them."

She punched him gently in the arm. He caught her fist and brought it to his lips, unclenched it, put her index finger in his mouth and circled it with his tongue.

"Let's sleep on it," she said in a dreamy voice.

"Or not." He zeroed in on her. "Will you puh-leez get rid of that laptop?"

"Will you puh-leez get rid of that hat," she said.

"Delighted to." He tossed it off. "Do you keep a shopping list?"

"Of course." She was folding her hat, laying it out on the nightstand.

"Put condoms on it."

12

Carter stalked into Maybelle's office Tuesday night and caught her going through what appeared to be a college catalog and wearing a speculative expression.

"Hey, Jack," she said, hastily stuffing the catalog into a drawer.

He glanced at the array of diplomas, took a second to wonder if she could possibly be thinking of an additional educational experience, then sat down and started talking. The first thing he talked about was Mallory's idea to determine what each plaintiff wanted and try to get it for them as a way of settling the case.

"She does sound like a real bright woman," Maybelle said.

She had that odd look on her face he'd noticed several times before. He'd given up trying to figure out what it meant. "She is," he said. "And I think she's starting to think I'm pretty bright, too." He ducked his head.

"What'd she say?" Maybelle sounded thrilled.

Carter paraphrased the compliment Mallory had given him about handling the witnesses well. He didn't want to sound like he was bragging.

"Hooray!" Maybelle shrieked when he'd finished. "Y'all wanted to make that little shift in your image and you jes' did it!" A relieved look crossed her face. "You don't need me no more."

"Actually, I still do."

Her face fell. Were his problems that boring? He frowned at her.

"My boss is still a problem." From the first, he'd been careful not to mention names. "He as much as asked me to cozy up to our opponent if I wanted to settle this case."

"Man or woman?"

"Woman."

"That's a plus, anyhoo." When Carter glared at her, she said, "Do you want to cozy up to the lady?"

"No."

"Then don't."

"I don't intend to."

"Good. We got that settled," Maybelle said, looking satisfied.

"We haven't got anything settled." Carter felt himself go red in the face. "The point is that the man as much as asked me to make love to the opposition. It's unethical. Unprofessional."

"Unlikely," Maybelle said.

"Very."

"'Count of you're hooked on this other girl."

"No, because it's unprofessional and unethical."

Maybelle snorted.

Carter folded his arms across his chest. "Sounds to me like you're more interested in her than you are in me."

"Which her?"

"The woman I...have some feelings for—to call it 'hooked' is going too far. I think you're looking for an easy answer to my problem."

She folded her arms across her chest to match his pose. "Mebbe that's because yore problem has an easy answer. Jes' open yore eyes, and mouth, while you're at it. Y'all go home and think about that for a while."

In short, from Carter's point of view, it was not a satisfactory session. Maybe it *was* time for Maybelle to go back to college.

WEDNESDAY EVENING HE stood in Phoebe's conference room reading the note Mallory had left him. "I'm going to find a suitcase. I'll be back at the hotel a little after eight."

He could not, absolutely could not believe Mallory could make love with him with such apparent pleasure and be seeing someone else. But he was holding evidence to the contrary right there in his hand. For the second time this week, she'd gone somewhere without him. He would have been happy to help her pick out a suitcase, but she hadn't invited him. *Ergo,* she had a life that didn't include him but might possibly include someone else. If the practice of law did nothing else for you, it taught you to be logical.

He was grinding his teeth, chewing his lower lip and fiddling with his pen all at the same time when a slight noise alerted him to the fact that he wasn't the only person in the office suite. He spun to see who'd stepped into the conference room and saw Phoebe behind him.

She'd taken off her jacket and was wearing a T-shirt that didn't have quite enough room in it for her breasts and didn't quite make it to the waistband of her very short skirt. Plus, she was sending him a provocative smile and gazing at him with sultry eyes.

Yep, I'm in trouble.

"Hi, Phoebe." He used his hearty tone, the one he used with women when he was trying to tell them he wasn't interested. "I'm just about outta here. See you in the—"

She was blocking his way. "Don't leave." Her voice was so soft it was hard to believe it belonged to Phoebe the lawyer. "I have a bottle of simply wonderful wine in my office. Come in and have a taste."

It occurred to Carter that he would have to confront the problem at one time or another, and it might as well be now, when he was a little bit mad at Mallory. "Okay, I will," he said. "Thanks."

The twenty-fourth floor was still brightly lighted, awaiting the services of the cleaning crew, except for Phoebe's office, where he observed at once that she'd dimmed the lights. *Big trouble.* She began to open the wine, not talking, just lifting her gaze to his between turns of the corkscrew and gazing at him like a snake might gaze at a mouse. Not that Phoebe looked like a snake or he felt like a mouse. It was just that he knew devouring him was what she had in mind.

He tried a little commentary on the weather.

"Mmm," she said.

He made mention of the political situation in the Middle East.

"Mmm," she said.

"How about that California state budget shortfall!" he tried next.

She didn't even bother with the "Mmm." She poured the wine, brought him a glass and sat on the arm of his chair, draping her arm around the back.

He got up. She followed, cornering him at the windows. He was thinking, *Twenty-four floors. A guy could get hurt pretty bad jumping twenty-four floors.*

Nonetheless, he opened the curtains, getting ready, just in case. The office looked out on a slice of the

Rockefeller Center Christmas tree, a Norway spruce well over one hundred feet tall and sparkling with maybe thirty thousand lights. It gave him an idea that was better than jumping. "It's almost Christmas," he said, and turned to face her. "What do you want for Christmas, Phoebe?"

She gazed at him with longing. "You," she said on a soft breath.

"What's your second choice?" He spoke as gently as he could.

She stared at him, and he was horrified to see that her eyes were brimming. "You mean, what do I really want out of life?" Her voice quavered.

He nodded dumbly, scared to death she was about to tell him.

"What I want is for my father, just once, to tell me I handled a case right," she stammered out. "All this—" she waved a hand at the wine, her tight T-shirt "—was his idea. I didn't want to do it this way. It's not the right way and, besides, anybody with two eyes can see you're in love with Mallory."

Carter handed her his clean breast-pocket handkerchief and one of Maybelle's cards, then stood there awhile, just patting her shoulder and asking himself if she was right. Was he in love with Mallory?

EACH MORNING MALLORY asked herself how life could be more perfect. At dawn on Thursday of their third week in New York, with Carter sleeping beside her, she knew how. He was still sneaking away a couple of times a week on this pretense or that. He didn't stay out late, he didn't come home mussed or go directly to the shower, he just—went out.

Of course, *she* was sneaking away, too. But she was

seeing Maybelle, which wasn't hurting Carter a bit. She'd seen Maybelle Monday night and last night at seven. Monday she'd told Carter she needed a manicure, and she and Maybelle had talked while she *did* have a manicure at Saks's Elizabeth Arden Salon.

Late yesterday afternoon she'd sneaked out of Phoebe's office while Carter was gathering some things together, leaving him a note saying she was going to buy a new suitcase and would see him at home. She'd picked out a suitcase in ten minutes and then taxied up to a boutique on the Upper East side where she and Maybelle had talked and selected two dinner dresses and two more jackets for Mallory.

"Variety is the spice of life," Maybelle had said.

"So I've heard." Mallory spoke through clenched teeth, predicting correctly that she was in for another of the bankruptcy nightmares that had been plaguing her.

"Not variety in everything," Maybelle had added, sounding unusually absentminded, "jes' in clothes."

So while she'd been as thoughtful of Carter as she could possibly be, on Tuesday night he'd said, "I have an errand to do. See you at eight."

He'd said it as if he didn't owe her an explanation, and, of course, he didn't. It was his reputation as a ladies' man that worried her. For all she knew, he saw her as just another of his string of women, while she

His face was toward her and she gazed at it, at the dark lashes that lay against his skin, the crispness of his tousled hair, and admitted to herself that if she hadn't already given him part of her heart, she wouldn't have been so determined to have sex with him. Had her feelings for him been locked up inside her, simmering, for all these years and she'd just now felt confident enough to let them out?

But Carter had never said he loved her or indicated in any way that he felt committed to their relationship. She had to face the possibility that he never would.

Except for that, she thought sadly, everything was perfect.

"Hi," he said in the husky voice of a man just waking up. His smile was slow, warm and altogether irresistible.

She settled her head down into her pillow. "Hi," she said as she felt his fingers trail lightly across her bare skin. Perhaps just having him committed to her for the next half hour was enough.

THE DELIGHTS OF THE early morning made it even more incomprehensible when he said offhandedly that evening, "I told a guy I knew in college I'd meet him for a drink. You don't mind if I skip out for a while, do you?"

The truth was that she minded terribly. As she fiddled with things on her desk, trying to stay busy while he was gone, the phone rang. It was Bill Decker, who spent a minute exchanging pleasantries with her and said at last that he needed to speak to Carter.

She didn't know why he would need to say something to Carter he couldn't say to her as well, but she didn't want to sound jealous or competitive, so she said, "He's not here just now, Bill. Frankly, I don't know where he is, but—"

Bill's chuckle interrupted her. "I think I can guess," he said.

"Where?" She snapped out the word.

"Okay, I'll level with you. Wasn't going to, thought

it might embarrass Carter, but I've been putting a bee in his bonnet about Phoebe Angell."

"Oh?" This time she managed to smooth out her voice. "What about Phoebe?"

More chuckles. She wished he'd choke and there wouldn't be anybody around who knew how to do the Heimlich maneuver. "In a conversation I had with her," he said when he apparently felt he'd chuckled enough, "it was clear she was interested in him. I suggested he pay a little attention to her, stroke her up a little."

"When he returns from stroking," Mallory said, feeling cold all over, "I'll ask him to give you a call."

She stood absolutely still for what seemed like an hour. Then she knew what she had to do. She had to see Maybelle. Maybelle would know it was an emergency. She'd find time for her in her schedule. Mallory flung on her coat and boots and went out into the night.

"YOU DONE GOOD, HON," Maybelle told Carter after he'd described his encounter with Phoebe. "You're a fine man and you did a kind thing. You followed your own conscience without hurtin' her any more than you had to. And—" she punctuated this by pointing a gold fingernail at him "—you found out what she wanted most in the world."

Carter was amazed at how good her compliment made him feel.

"And I been thinkin' about that All-I-Want-for-Christmas thing."

He didn't remember telling her Mallory's name for it, but he probably had. "All ideas appreciated," he said.

"I think this is a good one. You could produce a movin' pitcher or a sitcom with green people in it and cast all your witnesses, that is, if they're willing to settle."

Carter opened his mouth to explain how difficult, call it impossible, that would be, but he didn't need to explain a thing. Maybelle could handle both sides of any argument.

"But it turned out not to be setch a good idea. I talked to a movie person I know and he turned the idée down flat. The *concept,* he called it, didn't grab him, he said."

Carter's mind was clicking like a computer keyboard. "No, that idea was over the top," he said slowly, "but I think you've given me one that might work."

The rest of the session wasn't as productive. Maybelle seemed determined to make him admit he was in love with Mallory and furthermore to tell Mallory he was in love with her and see what she had to say about it, while he felt that if he was in love with Mallory it was none of Maybelle's business. Nor did he intend to make himself that vulnerable to Mallory until he was darned good and sure she was going to answer back, "I love you, too."

While he was arguing his point, he realized so unexpectedly that it was like being ambushed in a dark alley, that it would hurt—a lot—if he decided he was in love with Mallory and then found out she wasn't in love with him. That made him mad at the world in general, and in that mood, he wasn't open to any suggestion Maybelle was likely to make.

MALLORY RAN RECKLESSLY up to Maybelle's door. *New doorknocker.* A hand scrunched up like a fist as if it were about to knock. Mallory pounded it. Richard appeared. He seemed startled to see her. She breezed right past him anyway. "I need to see Maybelle. Just for a minute."

"She's with a client," he mouthed, pointing at the closed door and crossing two fingers over his lips.

"I'll wait."

"She really doesn't like her clients to meet," Richard said, obviously trying to edge her back out the door. "It's a privacy thing."

"I won't know the person," Mallory said, persisting. "I'm from out of town, remember? It'll be fine."

"I think not." Richard was getting pompous. "Here's what we'll do. You go home and Maybelle will call you the minute she's free."

"I can't go home," Mallory said. "I'm too upset."

She heard voices close behind the door. "Hear that?" she said. "They're almost finished. So I'm going to wait and that's—"

The door opened, and Carter stepped through it.

His eyes widened and his skin paled. Her heart fell to her toes. "What are you doing here?" she whispered.

"The question is," Carter said, "what are *you* doing here?"

The foyer fell into thunderous silence, but not for long. "Oh, my gawd, I knew this was gonna happen, I just knew it," Maybelle shrieked from somewhere behind Carter.

"I tried to send her home, Maybelle, truly I did," Richard said, looking woebegone. "But she's a very determined woman."

"You've been consulting Maybelle?" Mallory said to

Carter. "But why? And how did you find her?" However startled she was to see him, she was ecstatic to know he'd been seeing Maybelle and not Phoebe.

"You were the one who dropped that card in the hall, weren't you?" Carter said, but he didn't smile, and his voice was eerily calm.

"Whoo, what a relief," Maybelle said shrilly, scurrying out into the foyer. "Now you both know where the other one's been sneakin' off to, no place but to right here. No harm done. Isn't that grand? Now let's all sit down and have a little—"

"I don't want to sit down," Carter said. "I just want to know what you were consulting Maybelle about."

"Personal matters. Why were you seeing her?" She was merely curious. As far as she was concerned, Carter was perfect, didn't need to change a thing.

"Personal matters." He threw the words back at her.

He'd probably been as shocked to see her as she was to see him, but she didn't know why it was making him mad. "Oh, okay, I'll tell you," she capitulated. "There were some things about myself I thought I ought to change." Would she ever have the courage to tell him that she must have loved him even back in law school and that she badly wanted him to notice she was a woman? Even if she found that courage, she wouldn't say it here. Not in front of Maybelle and Richard.

"Uh-huh," Carter said. "I think I know why you consulted an imagemaker. A lot of things are coming together in my mind."

"What's comin' together?" Maybelle darted worriedly between Mallory and Carter.

"That's what the clothes and the shoes and the stuff—" Carter mimed makeup application "—and the mistletoe were all about. You asked Maybelle to change you from the woman you were into the woman who seduced me." He shook his head, looking sad. "I thought you were different, but you're not. You're just like all the rest." He turned away and appeared to be leaving.

"What do you mean, 'just like all the rest'?" This was just a silly little coincidence they should be laughing about. Instead, Carter seemed to be extremely upset and she couldn't figure out why.

He paused and turned back to her. "I thought you were starting to respect me because I was handling the depositions well, but you weren't really impressed by my legal skills. All you wanted was to get into my pants."

"Isn't it the woman who usually says that?" Richard asked Maybelle in a hushed tone.

"Shhh," Maybelle rasped back at him.

Carter turned on their mutual imagemaker. "In fact, you probably advised her to flatter me, that men were so egotistical they'd believe anything."

"No, she didn't," Mallory said, feeling desperate. "You did handle the witnesses well. I was being honest with you. I don't know what I did to make you so mad!"

"What's making me so mad," he said, giving her a humorless smile, "is being treated like an empty-headed gigolo. That's not what I am, and I wanted you, of all people, to know it."

"Empty headed..." She couldn't even follow his line of reasoning.

"What you did was deliberate, Mallory, a scheme from your clever little mind. I was hoping it came from the heart." He shook his head once sharply. "So it's over. From now on we are professional colleagues, nothing more."

Before she could gather her wits about her, he was out the door and on his way down the sidewalk. She ran to the door, too. "Wait just a minute," she yelled into the street. "What were *you* consulting Maybelle about?"

He was gone.

But Maybelle wasn't. "He wanted people to stop thinkin' of him as an empty-headed gigolo," she said in a despondent way that was totally unlike the Maybelle Mallory knew. "You're so smart you shoulda been able to figger that out for yourself. Dickie, I got to find me a new line of work. This one ain't givin' me any personal satisfaction and the money's real disappointin', too."

Mallory collapsed to the floor in tears. "Don't cry, hon," Maybelle said, scooping her up with amazing strength. "I ain't quittin' my job yet. Come on in and let's have us a cup of real coffee to calm us down. We'll think of somethin'. Don't you worry."

13

ON SATURDAY MORNING, the first day of Hanukkah and five days before Christmas, Carter lay in bed staring at the ceiling. All day yesterday he'd fought the sick feeling in the pit of his stomach as he did his best to carry on with the depositions. But that was all the fight he'd had in him. He could feel himself giving in to the—he guessed it was heartbreak.

He didn't know men got heartbreak. He thought they just got mad.

He reached over to his night table, picked up his pen between his fingers and felt a little better, but not much. For reasons he couldn't imagine, Mallory had changed from a steady, trustworthy woman to a manipulative one. He hadn't thought it could happen. He'd thought she was one of the most ethical human beings he'd ever known.

That was one of the things he'd liked about her.

Maybe she'd actually been mad that he hadn't gotten her a separate room and had decided to show him she knew what he'd really had in mind. Or maybe it had bothered her that he hadn't seen any problem with them being in the same room and she had set out to show him how wrong he'd been about her, that she wasn't "good old Mallory" anymore but a hot little number.

Try as he might, he couldn't have imagined Mallory

going to bed with a man she didn't respect. That was another thing he'd liked about her.

I love so many things about her.

No, loved. Past tense. He'd been wrong about her ethics, wrong about her need to respect the man she gave herself to, because it was clear she didn't respect him at all.

He needed to move out of this suite. The St. Regis was still fully booked, but New York had thousands of hotel rooms. He'd assumed they couldn't *all* be occupied by shoppers, theatergoers, and folks in town for a taste of a New York Christmas season.

But a blizzard had raged through the night. With all three airports socked in, all the hotels just might be fully booked. Where would he go? It didn't matter. He'd sleep on a bench in Grand Central station. He had to move.

But to move, he'd have to pack. To pack, he'd have to fold everything that was lying around and sort through a thousand scattered pieces of paper.

He'd reimburse Mallory for the ornaments she'd insisted on buying, but he was taking the tree. He'd leave her the mistletoe to remind her of the way she'd tricked him into that first kiss.

Because he was carting the tree out, he'd have to take a taxi. Of course, the taxis wouldn't be running today. The city would get the streets cleared by tomorrow, but it hardly seemed worth the effort just for the relief of getting away for a mere three days. A couple of weeks ago, when they were still speaking, they'd agreed to suspend the depositions for the holiday, go home to Chicago early on the twenty-third and start up again on the first Monday in January.

He'd have to find the hotel room himself. Brenda

wouldn't be back at the office until Monday. He'd have to figure out a way to get the tree from here to—wherever—without breaking its balls.

Or he could just lie here. That would be the easiest thing to do. Maybe Mallory would decide to move.

WEARING HER ORIGINAL black jacket and pants, Mallory sat cross-legged on her bed organizing her makeup and toiletries. Carter would probably make fun of her, call it *micro*-organizing, but it wasn't. Arranging lipsticks according to depth of pink was simply—organizing.

Anyway, he was the one who should move. All this was his fault. Since he didn't seem to be making the slightest attempt to do the right thing, however, it seemed she would have to pack all her clothes, old and new, and roll her suitcases through the snowy streets to her new hotel room, assuming she could find one.

She could end up homeless, sleeping in a doorway. Her eyes filled with tears.

She drew herself up. She was taking the Christmas tree with her and that was that. Furthermore, she'd thought of two ways she might do it. She'd buy an ornament box and tissue paper or bubble wrap, wrap each ornament individually and put it in the box, then carry the tree in her biggest Bergdorf's tote bag—she'd saved them all for reuse.

The other plan was somehow to shrink-wrap the tree, decorations and all, in plastic. She was certain it could be done. She just didn't know where to find the closest shrink-wrap machine. So she'd better stick with the plan she could implement all by herself.

Could she carry all that on foot? It sounded like a lot

of work, didn't it? Just to save herself three days of living with the silent, accusing presence of Carter?

She'd see how she felt after she finished *organizing*.

But what if it was micro-organizing? Why was she doing it? Her gaze dropped to the Ellen Trent book, remembering what Maybelle had said about locking up her heart until she got her house clean. It was time to give up the Ellen Trent system and make room for a life. Grimly she rose out of bed, carrying the book in two fingers, and dropped it in her wastepaper basket.

She couldn't say it made her feel good, just immeasurably better. Still, what was the purpose of getting a life if she couldn't have it with Carter?

There was also the question of what to do with the navy-and-white-striped shirt she'd bought. She'd intended to give it to him for Christmas if she succeeded in her plan, which she clearly hadn't done. Maybe Macon could wear it. She still had no idea what he was doing in Pennsylvania—except falling in love. Some people never changed. She almost wished she hadn't. With a deep sigh, she added the shirt to her open suitcase, and saw a tear drop onto the gift box.

The real problem was that Carter had been right. She *had* set out to seduce him. What he didn't know was that she'd done it because she loved him.

When the housekeeper arrived, Mallory peeked out to see if Carter was answering the door, and when she heard the sound of his shower running, she told the woman to start in her room first.

She went down to breakfast. Gazing blankly out the windows, she observed that the storm had blown itself out. It was now merely snowing, adding more to the piles that still covered the streets and sidewalks. With many thoughts running through her head, she broke one of her own cardinal rules—never use a cell phone in public—and called Maybelle's office. "There's not much point in seeing her again," she told Richard, "but I'd like to come in this afternoon and settle the financial matters. My usual weekend time? Four o'clock?"

"Oh, dear," Richard said, "she thought you wouldn't want to see her and gave the president a double appointment so they could dig a little deeper into anger management and verbal communication skills. Could you come at six?"

"Sure. Why not?" Nothing else would be happening in her life. She'd do her shopping first, then see Maybelle.

Her shopping list was on her PalmPilot. She went to it, wrote in "ornament box" and "bubble or other wrap." Scanning the rest of the list, she zeroed in on "condoms."

She erased it so violently that the top section of her stylus popped off and landed on another table in somebody else's oatmeal.

CARTER HEARD THE sound of a vacuum cleaner and speeded up the dressing process. When he'd pulled himself together, he warily stuck his head out into the sitting room. Not seeing Mallory anywhere, he came out more confidently. "I'm through in there," he told the housekeeper, who was dragging the vacuum cleaner out of Mallory's room. After giving the woman a wave, he stepped outside the suite.

The housekeeper had set a bag of trash just outside the door. Even Mallory's trash was neat. On top lay a book. Carter swiveled his head to read the title. *Efficient Travel* by Ellen Trent. Trent? A relative of Mallory's?

He picked it up. Stealing trash. That's what he'd

sunk to. Inside was a note that began, "Dearest daughter." Ellen Trent was Mallory's mother?

He took the book with him and went out into the snow, slogging along in search of one of those bookstores with a café where he could settle in with coffee and something unhealthy like a cinnamon roll. He had some reading to do.

"RICHARD?"

"Yes, Mr. Wright. Or I suppose I can call you Mr. Compton now."

"Sure, sure," Carter said into his cell. "Call me whatever you want to. I just wanted to confirm my three o'clock appointment today."

"Oh, dear," Richard said, "Maybelle thought you were too mad at her to want to see her again, so she gave the president a double appointment so they could go more deeply into—"

"The president?" Carter said.

"Not our president," Richard explained. "Another president. Anyway, she can't see you at three, but she could see you at six."

"Fine. I'll be there. Get my bill ready, okay?"

He got up from the spot he'd barely moved from since the café opened this morning. He'd only risen to refresh his food and beverage supply and track down a couple more Ellen Trent books. He felt cross-eyed from speed-reading and dizzy from carbohydrate overload.

And overwhelmed with insight.

He knew what was wrong with Mallory. Her mother was insane, that's what. That stuff about checking the expiration dates of everything in your house before you left on a trip—psychotic, in his opinion. No dirty laundry. When did you ever have *no* dirty laundry?

He felt newly sympathetic toward Mallory for growing up with an insane mother who'd taught her to be an automaton instead of warm and womanly.

He'd realized something else as well. Mallory had become warm and womanly. She'd given up most of the routines she'd been brainwashed into performing in order to make love with him. They'd eaten in bed, trashed the room, and he knew for a fact she hadn't cleaned off every scrap of her makeup, brushed her hair one hundred times and hand-washed her unmentionables every night before going to bed. He hadn't given her time. She'd bought those sexy clothes to snag him, yes, but she'd changed in other ways, too.

Was it possible she actually cared about him, or was her behavior an act of rebellion toward her insane mother, and he'd just been a convenient excuse to lose her inhibitions?

That was what he intended to talk over with Maybelle.

He had time to spare. Too much time. Aimlessly strolling along a newly cleared sidewalk, he caught sight of Bloomingdale's to the east and remembered the dress he'd spotted from the escalator on that first trip to the store to buy socks. When he'd suddenly wanted to kiss her. When his life had changed forever.

His pace quickened.

THE DARKNESS WAS thick and heavy at six o'clock. Muted street lights, tasteful Christmas displays and menorahs displaying two lighted candles shone through the tall windows of the town houses on the street, illuminating the deep snow and the flakes still falling from above. Mallory had her hand on Maybelle's new doorknocker when she heard footsteps on the sidewalk and spun to see Carter standing there, hesitating.

Without exchanging a word, he turned on one heel and started off to the east and she ran down the walkway and took off to the west. Maybelle tackled her at the corner, and when the dust cleared, she saw Richard propelling Carter back toward the mansion.

"You two," Maybelle scolded, "are gonna sit down and talk whether you want to or not. Kevvie," she screamed, "get that there door open before they get away!"

Mallory let herself be steered into Maybelle's office. Carter was digging in his heels, looking as if he'd like to take out Richard by slamming Kevin into his gut, not that he'd do something like that, but he looked furious enough to think about it. Two chairs sat in front of Maybelle's desk—a new and extremely conservative desk—and when their captors had deposited her and Carter into them, Maybelle sat down, flanked by Kevin and Richard, who were rocking from foot to foot, their hands clasped behind their backs, like bodyguards.

If nothing else, it was dramatic.

"What are you doing here, Kevin?" Carter was the first to speak.

Kevin relaxed his pose into a slump of despair. "I'm here because I feel as if I started all this," he said mournfully, gazing at Mallory, "by giving you Maybelle's card instead of just sticking to my ho-ho-hos."

"Naw, y'all was just lookin' after my bidness interests," Maybelle said. "I was the one started it by tawkin' her into sexy clothes and stuff instead of telling her just to let her insides show on the outside. I sent that there tree hopin' it'd warm her up a little—"

"You sent the tree?" Mallory and Carter spoke in

chorus. She darted a glance at him, saw he'd sent one toward her and quickly looked away.

Richard spoke up. "Well, I didn't start anything but coffee, which is what I'm going to do again. Now. Every conceivable kind of coffee," he snapped. "No need for custom orders."

"Bill actually started it," Mallory said with a stab of remembrance, "by appointing me to the case, but he's not to blame for anything. I am." She sighed and wrung her hands together. "I started it by deciding to catch Carter, make him see me as a woman, because—"

"I started it," Carter said abruptly.

Mallory swiveled her head to stare at him.

"I asked Bill to appoint you to the case."

From the distance came the whir of a coffee grinder, but Mallory's gasp was the only sound in the room.

"Why?" she said finally.

The gaze from his dark blue eyes was full of pain as it locked with hers. "Because I trusted you, for one thing. But the other thing, well, I wanted to show you I'd grown up. Prove to you I was a good lawyer. No, a great lawyer. A man you could respect."

"But I've always respected you," Mallory whispered. "All those years ago, I respected you for not giving up. You were always so smart, smart in ways I wasn't. But nobody ever expected good grades out of you, so you'd never learned to study. That's all I did for you, really, was show you that you could succeed."

"Whoa," Maybelle said. "Minute ago Mallory was about to say why she wanted you to see her as a woman. So. Why?"

Under Maybelle's compelling stare Mallory knew the moment of truth had arrived. "Because I think, even way back then in law school, that's what I really wanted."

"You did a great job of hiding it," Carter said suddenly. His voice was a fierce growl.

"I know." She tried to shrink her voice, tried to pretend she was hardly there. "I was afraid you'd reject me. Every woman I knew wanted you. Why would you ever choose *me?*" She sneaked a peek at him. The fierceness was fading from his expression, which gave her the courage to add, "All I meant to do here in New York was, well, stop hiding it."

"An', Carter," Maybelle went on inexorably as if the tension in the room wasn't already close to explosive, "why'd y'all care what Mallory thought of you?"

"I guess it had always been a sore point thinking she saw me as a dumb jock who couldn't have made it through law school without her," he mumbled. Now his eyes were downcast.

"But why was it a sore point? Come on, Carter, am I gonna have to get out my sledgehammer?" Maybelle's voice rose sharply.

"Because..." Now he sounded a little desperate. "Because I..."

"Keep goin' hon," Maybelle said. "You'll get there evenshully."

"Because I...liked her."

"You did?" Some sensation flooded through Mallory—either relief, or building desire, or maybe it was just that simple affection she'd felt that afternoon in New York when all he was doing was getting into a football game.

Out of the corner of her eye, Mallory saw Kevin quietly leave the room. She was focused on Carter, though, who was giving her a defensive look and shifting uncomfortably in his chair.

"Yes, I did," he said.

"I wish I'd known," Mallory said. "All I knew—" she was embarrassed to feel tears rising into her throat "—was that I was the only woman in law school you never came on to. Even when we spent the night alone in your apartment."

"'Scuse me," she barely heard Maybelle say.

"I wanted to kiss you that night," he said, and she saw the beginnings of a crooked smile, "but I didn't think you wanted me to, and I was trying to act like one of the good guys."

Mallory got up, tired of this side-by-side conversation when the things she had to say were the most important things she would ever say in her whole life. Carter got up, too, looking appealingly nervous. "Carter," she said gently, "if you'd kissed me that night, I would have made love with you right there on the desk on top of *Roe v. Wade.*"

Now he seemed stunned. "You would have?"

Mallory sighed. "Probably not. I probably would have filed *Roe v. Wade* first, in a file labeled *Roe v. Wade.*"

They gazed at each other for a long, long moment, suddenly aware they were alone in the room now.

Carter said, "I could have handled that." He moved close to her, folding his arms around her, holding her tight, his face buried in that sensitive spot just under her ear. "I could probably have handled it if you'd checked the expiration date on my condoms first." She jolted in his arms. "Oh, Mallory," he said, "can we start over now that we have full disclosure?"

"No way." She searched for his mouth with hers. "It

was too tough the first time around. Let's call that the cross-examination. Now we make our closing statements." She found his mouth at last, or he found hers. Who knew, who cared? All that mattered was that they'd found each other.

"LET'S TALK SETTLEMENT," Carter said to Phoebe when they'd trapped her in her office Monday morning.

"We're going to trial."

"Phoebe, I've done a lot of research on these kinds of lawsuits and going to trial is a big gamble," Mallory said. "Even when the plaintiffs win, they often don't win enough to make them happy."

"Settlement is in your clients' best interests and in yours," Carter added. "That was the judge's opinion after reviewing the items of evidence and reading through the court reporter's transcript to date. You were there. You heard him."

Phoebe's lips tightened. "You don't understand. I have to go to trial. I have to win. I have to prove..." She stared at the wall behind Mallory and Carter where the portrait of her father hung.

"You don't have to prove anything to your father," Mallory said quietly.

"How would you know anything about my father and what I do or do not have to—"

"Because I have a mother. Have you ever heard of Ellen Trent?"

"Everybody's heard of Ellen Trent. Martha Stewart minus the charm."

Mallory winced. "The very same."

"She's your mother."

"Yes."

"If you settled a case when she'd told you to hold out for trial—"

"She'd disown me."

"And you wouldn't care."

"I'd care. But I'd still do what I knew was right." Under the apron of the desk, Mallory crossed her fingers.

"In fact," Carter said, "you don't have to work with your father."

Phoebe's olive skin paled, but with her remaining bravado, she said, "Of course I don't *have* to. I work with him because—"

"You work with him because he convinced you you'd never get a job anywhere else."

"He did not!"

"Not in so many words."

She crumpled. "I guess he did."

"He's wrong," Carter said. "You're good at your work. Terrific at your work." He smiled broadly. "Look what you put us through."

"You really think—"

"I absolutely know. I would be more than happy to write a letter of recommendation to my firm on your behalf—"

Mallory kicked him.

He gave her a look. "—for a position at the San Francisco branch of Rendell and Renfro," he said distinctly, still looking at Mallory. "I hear they're looking for a couple of experienced and super-sharp lawyers."

Mallory held her breath through a lengthy silence. At last, with a look of steely determination in her eyes, Phoebe said, "Okay, what's your offer?"

Mallory swallowed the whoosh of air that emerged involuntarily from her lungs. Carter handed Phoebe several stapled sheets of paper. "This is a summary of the offer. The full document is being prepared right now and you'll have it by this afternoon."

"As you can see," Carter went on, not sounding at all like a man who'd been up all night working on that document, "we're offering restitution in the amount of damages, doubled. You get half, the client gets half."

Phoebe nodded, then looked up. "What in the world is this bit about a demo tape?"

"We looked over the transcript and observed that a majority of your clients had aspirations such as show business or modeling. Not surprising in New York, when you think of it."

Phoebe nodded.

"Sensuous is offering each interested client the opportunity to have a demo tape made. It will be professionally filmed and directed, something Kevin's agent can use to get auditions for him, something Mrs. Ross can use to get an agent for little..."

Mallory supplied him with the baby's name, which she remembered from the interrogatories.

Carter's head swiveled toward her. "Desiree? Did she really name that baby Desiree?"

"Carter..." She hummed a warning.

He cleared his throat. "Little Desiree," he said calmly. "God bless her."

Phoebe was quiet again, reading. "I'll take this offer to my clients and see what they think of it." She granted them a slight smile, her gaze going back and forth between them. "Maybe you'll have more than one thing to celebrate before you go home for Christmas."

"COULD WE HAVE OUR OWN private Christmas tonight?" Carter asked her during the walk back to the hotel.

They were both dragging along, tired but victorious, clinging to the good feeling that they'd done their best and everybody had won. "I'm not up to a huge celebration," Mallory said, proving her point with a huge yawn, "but a little champagne around the tree would be nice. It's our last night in the suite," she added with heartfelt regret. "Home to Chicago tomorrow. The first thing I'll have to do is go through the mail—"

"The first thing you have to do is spend the night in my apartment," Carter instructed her.

"Okay. That way I won't feel as if I've actually gotten any mail."

"And we won't mess up your apartment."

"Good point."

"Then it's my parents for Christmas Day," Carter said.

"After mine for Christmas Eve." She'd thought that of the two options, her mother's frozen oyster stew on Christmas Eve would be preferable to her frozen turkey on the day itself. "Try not to scatter anything around while you're there," she said. "And remember, no shoes in the house, and after you shower, you're supposed to wipe down the tile."

"I'll be on my best behavior," he promised. "Don't you think your mother will be flattered that I read her book?"

"Until you tell her what you thought about it," Mallory said.

"I would never! Would I ever?" he protested. "Will I get to meet the invisible Macon?"

They'd spent a lot of time the day before just getting to know each other, telling childhood stories, discussing their parents' eccentricities. Mallory laughed. "He finally answered my last e-mail this morning. He was doing a top secret job in Pennsylvania, where he met a woman who'd never laid fingertips on a computer—"

"No!" Carter said.

"But she has now." She glanced up at him. "There's a possibility, a strong possibility, that she might come to Chicago with him. Carter, I think the Trent kids have finally grown up."

Carter looked thoughtful for a minute, then turned his heartstopping smile on her. "So has the Compton kid."

"And beautifully, I must say," Mallory said.

They reached the suite. "I'm going to slip into something more comfortable," she told him.

"How about bed?"

"Champagne around the tree, remember?"

She came back wearing her pink gown and robe, carrying the box with Carter's shirt inside, and noticed that he was sitting on the sofa holding an identical gift box. She stopped short. "When did you buy me a present?"

"Saturday."

"You couldn't have Saturday. We came right home after—"

"I bought it before we met at Maybelle's," he said, standing up to take her in his arms.

She clasped her hands around his neck. "I bought yours that first day at Bloomingdale's," she said, one-upping him quite nicely, she thought.

He smiled at her. "Never said you weren't smarter than I am. Let's open them now."

"Just like a kid," she teased.

"Yeah, because I think I know what mine is." He

ripped open the package and pulled out the striped shirt. "How can I afford you if you're going to buy me designer shirts?" he grumbled.

She could tell he was pleased, but her attention was focused on the champagne-colored dress she'd pulled out of its box. It was exquisite, slender and clingy, and if she were not badly mistaken, it matched her hair exactly. "Carter, it's beautiful," she breathed.

"So are you." He took her in his arms. "You were beautiful in those sweaters you used to wear in law school, the great big ones that hung down almost to your knees."

"Oh, no, I wasn't."

"I didn't say sexy." When she tried to pummel him in the stomach, he said, "But I—"

She stopped trying to pummel him and looked up into his eyes. "Liked me anyway?" she whispered.

"Loved you anyway," he said against her cheek.

His kiss left her breathless. "We can try on our new clothes in the morning."

"At the earliest."

Still she struggled a little in his arms. "We really should call Maybelle and tell her what happened today." She drew back to look at him pointedly. "I think we'd better do it now, if you intend to kiss me like that again."

"You dial. I'll pour champagne."

She dialed. The telephone rang three times, after which a recorded message came on. "You have reached the offices of Events by Ewing, razzle-dazzle parties in no time flat. Ms. Ewing can be reached during regular office hours, which are..."

Stunned, she put down the phone. "Event planner," she muttered.

"Aw, Mallory," Carter said plaintively, handing her a glass of pale bubbles, "do we have to have that kind of wedding? The kind you get an event planner for? I thought you were going to call Maybelle."

"We drove her out of business," Mallory said. "Strongest woman I've ever known and we ended her career."

"What are you talking about?"

When would she stop falling in love with him all over again every time she looked at him? Never, probably. All of a sudden she realized he'd said the magic words. He'd said *love,* and he'd said *wedding*. She put down her glass, threw her arms around him and said, "Don't bother your pretty head about it. I'll explain it to you in the morning, darling."

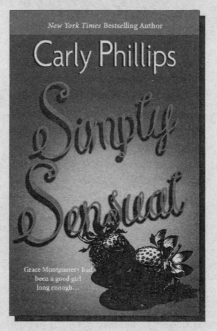

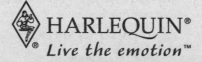

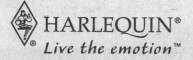